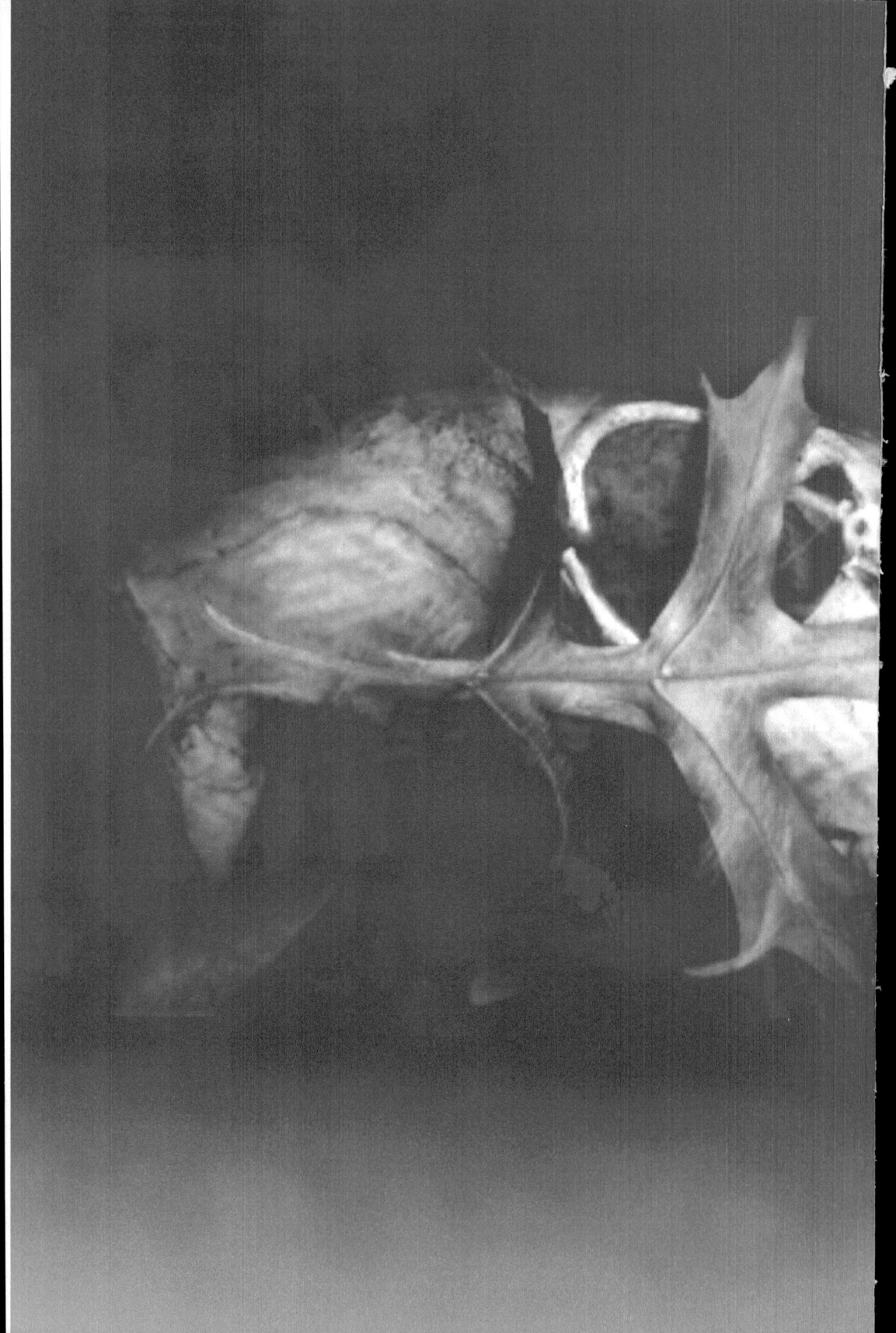

# THE
# GOLDEN ROAD

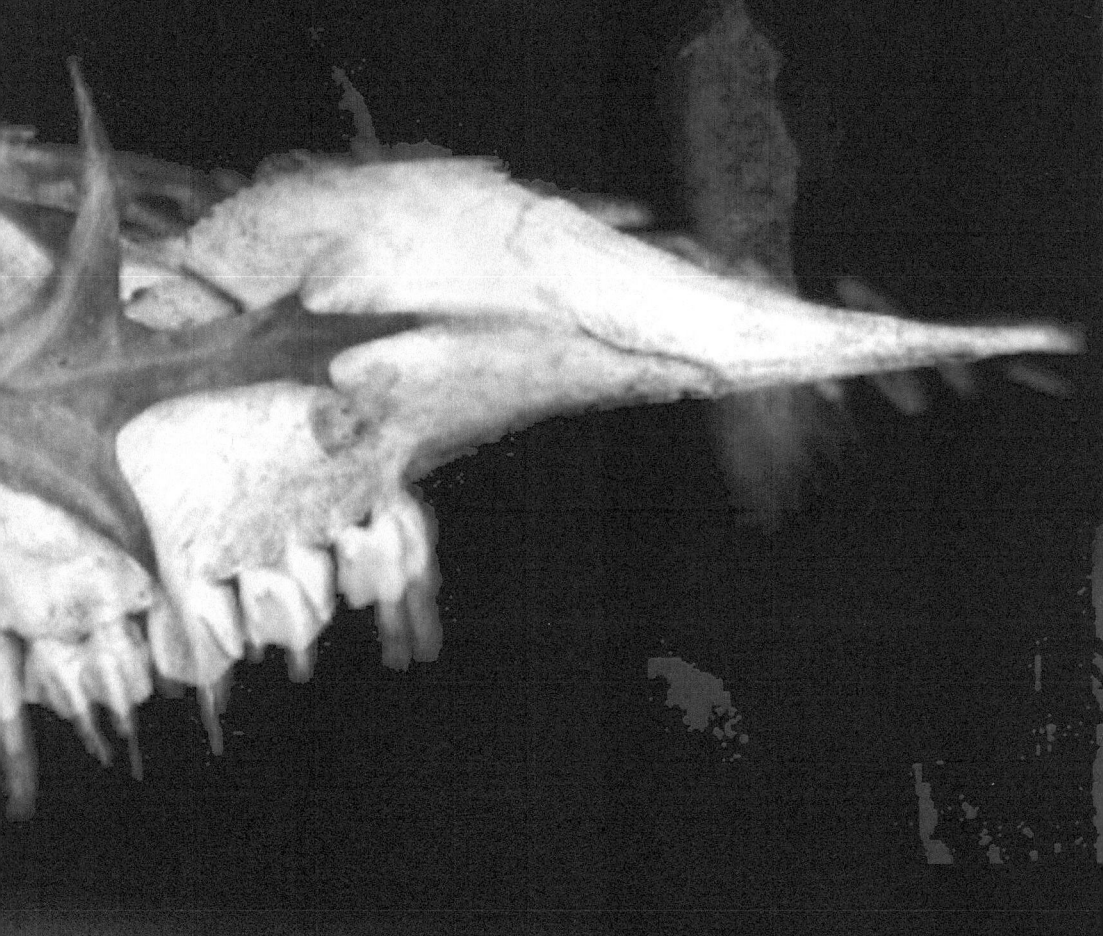

Selene dePackh

ISBN: 978-1-68510-019-3 (sc)
ISBN: 978-1-950305-68-1 (ebook)
Library of Congress Catalog Number: 2022931590

First printing edition: February 25, 2022
Published by JournalStone Publishing in the United States of America.
Cover Design and Layout: Selene dePackh
Edited by Sean Leonard
Proofreading and Interior Layout by Scarlett R. Algee

JournalStone Publishing
3205 Sassafras Trail
Carbondale, Illinois 62901

JournalStone books may be ordered through booksellers or by contacting:
JournalStone | www.journalstone.com

*For Suzanne, who makes it all possible.*

# THE GOLDEN ROAD

# I

# PRAYER FOR DELIVERANCE

STEPHANIE ST. GILES tried to convince herself that the black lump on the roadside caught in the beam from her headlights hadn't been moving. She pulled her battered pickup off the right-of-way onto the berm of packed ice, but not far enough to risk sliding into the deep, snow-hidden drainage ditch running beside it. The rutted fire access track she used as a shortcut was barely visible under fresh drifts, marked only by the swath it cut through the scrubby trees. Low, hardened snowbanks allowing for the width of an emergency vehicle were mounded on either side, punctuated by an occasional reflective utility marker sticking through, shining in the distance as the track receded into the darkness ahead.

It was the start of Maine's legendary mud season, less than two weeks until spring, and the thawing ground was treacherous. A fierce flash of icy wind had left a deceptively solid-looking crust on the surface, but underneath lurked a thick layer of half-frozen muck. Flakes were coming down fast enough to make Stephanie want to keep the inspection short. The dark thing made her back prickle worse the more she looked at it.

She'd promised her friend Sylvie she'd take the better-traveled Golden Road out of Millinocket headed west, and then backtrack along the maintained gravel route to her cabin. The snow seethed softly against the truck's windshield. Hesitating a moment with the phone in her hand, she called Sylvie as she'd promised she would anytime something came up while she was out alone. It meant she'd have to confess to taking the shortcut.

Sylvie was another solitary, eccentric, not-quite-geriatric woman with whom Stephanie had recently, cautiously renewed a long-ago friendship. They'd been too prickly in earlier years to stay close, and had finally fallen out because of a painful incident they'd agreed not to discuss this time around. At the time, those years ago, they'd fought so bitterly that Stephanie thought they'd never speak again.

Age had forced both of them to become more circumspect as it moved from snapping at their heels to sinking its teeth in. Not long after Stephanie had reconnected with Sylvie, they made a pact to look out for each other. Part of that agreement entailed phoning in when either one of them was on the road and had to stop for any reason. Stephanie sometimes wondered which one of them found the arrangement more annoying.

"Damnit, Steve... What now?" The reception was clear enough for Stephanie to hear the panicky reproach in Sylvie's tone. "How many times have I pleaded with you—don't take that godforsaken track where there's no one around for miles! What were you thinking!?"

Stephanie tried to make a joke about seeing what might be a bag with body parts in it. Her voice came out more jazzed than she intended.

It didn't go over well. Sylvie said it sounded like she was dissociating again. Dissociation was one of Stephanie's post-traumatic veers and skids, but Sylvie could usually interrupt the derailments. As a home healthcare RN and vet tech serving a region in a decades-long economic depression, Sylvie had seen her share of desperate human beings.

When they rode together, it was always in Sylvie's SUV. Stephanie didn't invite anyone into her truck, which hadn't seen a cleaning rag since she'd bought it more than a decade ago. The first time she'd lifted their shopping bags into the SUV's immaculately vacuumed hatch, she'd noted a Ladies' Emergency Kit of pink-handled half-sized tools, including a hatchet and bowsaw, and asked if Sylvie thought she might have to be ready to build a fire to survive once she got out of sight of a streetlight. They'd driven in heavy silence for a few miles, the old prickles pushing them to lean away from each other against their respective doors. Then Sylvie had put on *You Want It Darker*, still poignant and new, and the two of them mourned and connected again over the shared loss of the poet who'd left it as a goodbye.

Now, Stephanie had no idea what she was feeling, other than being vaguely aware of shoving something down so she could do what she had to, and that her pulse was pounding in her ears. That wasn't anything she wanted to talk about, but she hung on the sound of the throaty, French-Canadian-accented voice admonishing her from a tidy living room in town.

"Steve—deep breath. Remember what you need to do when you get anxious. Organize your thoughts. Break the task down. List your objectives."

*So*, Stephanie thought, *objective one accomplished*. She was safely stopped. She cleaned her glasses on the hem of her flannel shirt. Sylvie's words crackled and faded in the empty miles of scrub timber regrowth between Millinocket and the truck. Stephanie wiped at the smudged safety-orange phone cover as if that might help the reception, and then slipped the silent device into her pocket without disconnecting the call in case Sylvie was still on the line.

Reluctantly, she concluded the rifle on the rack behind her head would be in her way. Carrying a firearm slung on her back while on slippery ground and leaning on a pikestaff, possibly needing to use her free hand quickly, didn't calculate out to be the safer choice. The spiked walking stick would have to be weapon enough.

Attempting to appear less recognizably female to anyone who might be watching, she tucked her long, gray braid under her watch cap, stepped from the cab, and flicked on her flashlight.

*Objective two, done.*

Gripping her trekking pole, she reached in the loose waistband of her jeans and snugged the spica wrap around her bad hip in case she had to move in an arthritic sixty-ish woman's version of fast. Her kid-sized Timberland work boots with thick, businesslike treads were losing traction on the compacted ice, now covered with a fresh layer of powder as slick as talcum. Osteoporosis wouldn't be kind to her wrists and pelvis if she slipped. Falling snow sparkled in the beam she aimed at the dark blob. A couple of cautious steps closer showed something she tried harder and harder to convince herself was a sack of rubbish.

Objective three was presenting a challenge. A pebble formed in her throat as she made out sweeping curves freshly carved in the snow.

She forced out a questioning "Hello?" from her tightening vocal cords.

A muffled wailing answered, and the shape repeated the thrashing that had cut into the snow. A sickle-line of red marked the arc of the slice.

Sylvie's jagged voice from Stephanie's pocket almost made her lose her grip on the flashlight. "What [sputter]…going…Steve? Are…there?"

The creature slid away toward the ditch. Stephanie gimped to it in time to grab a powerful foreleg as it flailed its hindquarters until its broken, bloodied nails caught in the gouged ditch bank. It pushed itself partway onto the shoulder.

"It's a dog, Syl." Stephanie shone the light into a pair of glowing eyes. "A motherfucking *huge* dog. Can't even tell what color, it's so covered in gunk. It looks…" The beam caught thick, filthy-wet fur over heaving ribs. The animal raised a hind leg to show her rescuer her smeared belly and wagged her sodden tail weakly. "…thought it was hit but—jeezus, its mouth is taped—wire around the front paws at the wrist… Oh, baby girl, who did this to you?"

A thing in the back of her mind already knew the answer to that. Reality began to recede, and she fought to keep her mind focused.

The animal lay on her side, the tip of her tongue lolling a fraction of an inch out of her bound jaws into the slush. Her nostrils were partly blocked by the melting muck.

Without thinking, Stephanie cleared the stuff away.

The dog was soaked in composted-vegetable-matter soup starting to collect a frosting of snow. It looked as though she'd been dumped into the steep-sided ditch and had used all her strength to pull and claw her way out with her forearms wired together. She was fading with the exhaustion of struggling to keep from sliding back in.

Her distended teats suggested she'd recently whelped. A queasy, lightheaded feeling washed over Stephanie as she recognized the trade practices of a venture she thought, or hoped, she'd left behind half her life ago. She floated in numbness. The only thing unfamiliar was that the animal wasn't dead.

"Stephanie, listen to me!" Sylvie sputtered in her ear. "Do not try to touch…tape off, leave…wire…wait…get there. You know as…injured anim…dangerous. Steve!! Steve?"

"You're breaking up, Syl. I have to get her warm. Meet you at the clinic."

"Fuck you, Steve. You're…I'll be there in…pray for you…owe Ste. Anne a novena for all…worrying I do about you. Drive sane, okay?"

Stephanie put the phone back in her pocket. The dog wouldn't be getting in the pickup without her own help. Pulling off her gloves with her teeth and then holding the torch in her mouth, Stephanie pointed the light at the twisted wire cutting deep into heavy-boned forelegs. She knew there was a good chance she'd been intended to pull over and find what she did. She pictured the rifle behind the seat, but it was too late to regret the choice.

The bitch shoveled her duct-taped muzzle under Stephanie's arm, watching as she forced her stiff fingers to untwist the heavy-gauge copper. The wire had sliced so far into flesh that the tendons shimmered as it unwound. It came away coated in blood.

The animal's upright ears were cold as the hardening ground, and she'd probably lose the edges to frostbite if she lived. She growled softly as her rescuer made soothing noises. She didn't whimper though, seeming to have the stoicism of a creature familiar with pain. Stephanie was glad for the tape; if those teeth were as formidable as the rest of the beast, they could make a mess of a skinny old woman.

Once Stephanie got the dog free, she threw the wire into the ditch. Waves of shivering surged through the lanky animal as she struggled to get to her feet. After a lot of flailing, Stephanie got the beast pulled up into her lap across her knees, long, muscular legs splayed out and trembling. The dog was able to support about half her own substantial weight.

*Objective number whatever, something or other.*

Stephanie looked into the dog's dilated eyes. "This is going to be interesting, gal. I won't be able to do shit for you unless we work together, and I need to get the hell out of here."

With a hard exhale, she killed the flashlight and pulled her gloves on. The truck seemed a football field away. The bitch nuzzled along Stephanie's jaw, seemingly in gratitude, *or,* she thought, *maybe checking for my jugular.*

Carefully cupping her hand over the top of the taped muzzle, Stephanie firmly pushed it back a few inches. A low tail-wag confirmed that the beast accepted the statement of boundaries.

Planting her staff, Stephanie hauled herself up to a high kneel, hooked her other arm around under the animal's chest, and they crawled. They both limped badly, and Stephanie wondered how long the circulation to those massive front paws had been cut off.

By the time they reached the truck, beast was pulling human more than the other way around. The dog knew what a vehicle was, clambering into the grimy footwell as soon as Stephanie opened the passenger door.

It was as if the animal had come home after a long time lost. Curling her big body tight on the floor next to the heat vent, she nosed at her shredded front legs.

Stephanie dragged her gunk-smeared self into the driver's seat. She locked the doors and then laid her head on the steering wheel, shut her eyes, and tried to make her teeth stop chattering. Her hip had to be functional so she could drive, and the spasms were forcing tears out of her.

The dog stood. Black sludge released its own fragrance over wet fur. Her pale gold eyes were startling against it. Common knowledge advises not to stare directly at a strange canine, but for this animal, Stephanie knew the advice was bullshit. The dog wanted to know who this person was who'd saved her, and that meant they needed to look into each other.

Stephanie took the glove off again and put her hand out. "Soon as I pull myself together, we'll get that mess off your face. I'm not going to hurt you."

The bitch sniffed Stephanie's fingers, then snuffled her nose down her side, planted her snout against Stephanie's bad hip and breathed warm into it like she was reading the scream coming from the disintegrating joint. It might have just been the compassion, but it helped.

Wiping her hand on her pants after she smoothed the animal's mucky head, Stephanie gave herself a fast pep talk, then put the truck in gear, turned around at the bottom of the private road where her cabin was, and aimed for the bright lights of downtown Millinocket.

Jake Ferguson cursed as he woke. Dozing off was the last thing he'd wanted to do. Sleep had seemed to pull him into itself like a vacuum. The void didn't want to let him back up into the real world, and he struggled to orient himself.

The truck cab was so cold his breath had obscured the windshield, the fog freezing into a fragile layer of fan-patterned crystals that caught a faint glimmer of ruby. Taillights crept away from the spot on the narrow, unplowed dirt road he'd been watching. Receding red pinpoints were all he could make out through the frost.

That was right, but also wrong. He blinked the blear from his eyes and reset his thoughts.

He'd waited hours to make sure the correct person would find what he'd left on the roadside, and now he couldn't be certain his setup had worked. The vehicle might not even have completely stopped. A drone behind the seat was useless, the weather too harsh to risk flying it. No choice but to haul himself out into the night. He hesitated and then took a hard pull from the pint of Canadian in his glove box. His blood began to warm up.

After the lights completely disappeared, he emerged from his truck, swearing silently at his uncooperative body. His legs were stiff, and the cold bit at them where they were moist from his body heat against the seat. He stepped cautiously out from behind the road grader that concealed his vehicle in the municipal pull-off.

The outside didn't offer much more detail. Barely able to see his feet, he shuffled in the dark through a quarter mile of silent, thickening snow. The crystalline fluff layering onto the access road would eventually both reveal and erase information around his handiwork.

As he passed a driveway leading up to a few hunting cabins, Jake removed his gloves and fumbled thick-fingered for a keychain Maglite. When he flicked it on, the falling snow shimmered in the pool of strong light hovering in the darkness. He noted no tire tracks leading uphill and no glow in the windows above. Some of the hilltop camps were only used seasonally, some were even more or less abandoned, but he knew one that wasn't. Instead, softening lines showed a vehicle had turned around there at the bottom of the slope, reversing direction to return to town. He smiled to himself.

Where he'd left his message to his ex-wife, there was a mess of pink-and-black-smudged gashes in the white drifts, gradually blurring in the fresh snowfall. Huge canine paw prints were smeared but unmistakable. Beside the place someone had parked for long enough to leave a shallow rectangular depression, there were a few disappearing tracks of heavy-treaded boots small enough for a boy.

Sylvie Antoine-Labbot extended her open palm to the dog, who shied from the overture. "Pups usually love me 'cause I'm built like a fire hydrant." She winked at the beast who was cringing against Stephanie while bristling aggressively.

Rubbing her close-cropped scalp to short-circuit a brewing headache, she sighed. "Looks like you've found yourself a new family member there, Steve. The attachment process appears to have begun—the clamps are on and the glue is already beginning to set. No signs she's seen the benefit of much domestication. I expect you know as well as I do she's likely to have a screw loose from conflicting instincts. She should fit right in."

The trembling canine crawl-limped forward under the fluorescent glare, eyes darting along the stainless steel and white laminate, her streaming nose sniffing franticly at the animal body fluid smells overlaid with disinfectant. Her battered, untrimmed nails slid on the waxed linoleum, leaving muddy, red-streaked smears. She squatted, urinating a quickly spreading puddle on the floor. Leaning on her cane to look down at the mess, Stephanie murmured an apology and something about needing a sanitary wipe.

"Don't worry about the pee, happens all the time," Sylvie said, reaching for a wad of coarse brown paper towels from the wall dispenser. "That lake's a few gallons too much to be dabbing with a sani-wipe. Grab the bleach spray." She nodded toward a gray laminate cabinet. "Good thing Darrow hardly comes into the office anymore. I've started handling his surgeries—his hands shake too much now. He's not going to complain if I use the facility for personal work—he trusts me to cover for him and his drinking." She lapsed into French as she tried to fill the awkwardness with reassuring jabber. Stephanie wasn't fluent in anything but redneck Mainer, so out of touch with her heritage that she'd even anglicized the pronunciation of her own last name, just like the idiot governor. Sylvie put the brakes on herself thinking about Paul LePage; that was never a good idea if she wanted to keep her blood pressure down. Deep breath. Never mind, Stephanie was a decent person and Sylvie reminded herself not to take it personally.

The dog had produced a thickly fragrant pool that threatened to escape into loosened gaps in the baseboard caulking. Sylvie had learned to push down revulsion at body fluids long ago, but this was threatening to kick up a retch. From her knees, she threw a wad of crumpled towels at the advancing stream and managed to dam the flow before it got into places she couldn't reach to clean.

She realized she was starting to mutter. Other people tended to take that badly, particularly once she drifted into mixing her languages. It was a small thing, in her opinion, but it earned her complaints to management from clients. She didn't want to risk spooking the only real friend she had left.

Rising painfully to her feet, she grabbed onto the edge of the examining table, and then bleached where she'd touched. She flipped the paddles on the faucet with her elbows and sighed as she lathered her hands. The foam sparkled between her fingers. She heard the bubbles laughing pleasantly.

*Cleanliness next to godliness, even if you won't believe in the Nobodaddy whose heel you grew up under. The Mothers and Sisters tried to make you grow twisted, but you matriculated clean anyway.*

Smiling to herself, she remembered not to repeat that out loud.

When she'd go to her court-mandated appointment with the psychiatrist in Bangor every six months, he'd look at her skeptically when she said she didn't see the things she saw, or heard what she heard. She knew what to say and not say to avoid another involuntary commitment.

The shrink did approve when he learned she had managed to renew and so far keep a genuine friendship.

This was going to be a whole new level of testing that.

"Steve, you're damned good with feral animals, good enough to know your limits." She pulled off Stephanie's tattered jacket to throw in the laundry, holding it away from herself by one of the few spots that showed an unsullied bit of faded tan canvas. "Take that couch-pillow off. You have to be sweltering."

Starting the washing machine as she spoke, she put her hand out for the down vest and then hung it on a peg by the back door, next to a man's heavy raincoat. "You do understand what you've got here? If you're willing to take her on, I'll help any way I can. If not, we should put her down now."

Stephanie turned to the animal cowering at her feet. "She's a wolf hybrid, right down to the weird, bifurcated behavior…and yeah, I can't just write her off."

"Yep. We'll see what we're dealing with when she's washed off. I'll put her in my novena for the vernal equinox. However it works out, I'll ask for kindness for her. She sure looks like she needs it. Now—are you game to tinker around that set of chompers if I give her a happy shot, or do you want her under? It'll be easier to get her clean if she can stand on her own."

"What do you think, lady?" Stephanie eased herself stiffly to the floor. "You gonna let me work on you without taking my hand off?"

The wolf dog forced her nose under Stephanie's armpit, hiding from the needle approaching her shoulder. It looked like she knew what an injection was. She flinched, breathed faster and then relaxed, sliding down so she rested her front half in Stephanie's lap.

Sylvie chuckled.

*She's easy. Man, I wish I could get off that smooth. I might consider ingesting pharmaceuticals if they worked that good on me.*

She tapped Stephanie's arm. "Lookie here." The fur was almost pure white where she'd cleaned the injection site. She felt goosebumps coming up, like the world was coming into an uncanny synchronicity. Those were perilous moments, but also the richest ones of her life—the ones she could never speak of. "You watch samurai movies?"

Her friend murmured a negative.

Sylvie dove into the swirling current. "*Lady Snowblood*. The one the *Kill Bill* ones were based on. Lead character was named Shura Yuki."

Jake looked out the partly snow-obscured casement window in his basement apartment. It butted up against stained ceiling tiles at the top of the paneled cinderblock wall, letting in the smudged amber glow of sodium lights in the parking lot. Another six inches had collected on his truck. Rolling over, he worked on falling asleep again. He'd told his new boss he might not be there for the morning rounds if he got in late from the run he had to make for his side job. Old-school Mainers respected hustle. He didn't expect crap when he made the announcement, and he didn't get it.

It wasn't even that much of a lie. He'd said he was bringing in a breeding bitch to a buyer from the kennel he was a partner in. The kennel was a convenient cover, but it was legal, as was the wildlife rehabilitation refuge connected to it. The bitch happened to be in an area of operations that wasn't on any official books, but it was true he was bringing her to someone. The buyer just didn't know she was going to get the animal, or how much she'd pay for it.

Yellow eyes stared at Jake as soon as he started drifting off.

His hands and forearms ached. The nameless wolf/malamute bitch had been vicious from the start, and he'd been ready for her. Even so, while he was preparing her for the tableau, she'd left him with bites that had bruised him through his Kevlar gauntlets. The result had been worthwhile; the creativity and relentless logic of the setup were elegant, but would hit like a sledgehammer. Thinking on that eased his bruises.

Malamutes are a breed prone to attacking humans, turning on them even after trust has apparently been established. That was part of the calculus. The hybrid's lupine blood would only amplify that unpredictable ferocity. There were so many ways it could work out.

*Almost three decades, but Justice will be done, one way or another.*

After what the monster had done to her own offspring, he was confident of her savagery. He'd been anticipating the new litter, expecting the exorbitant stud fee to pay out more than enough dividends to make it worthwhile. The stud had been out of his own stock, and he'd regretted selling him even for the price he got. The bitch was arguably the finest animal he'd ever produced, even if her temperament was ugly. Though she might not be fully physically mature, she was strong and enormous—certainly able to handle the strains of pregnancy. It would have been a waste to let her first heat pass without breeding her.

When the truculent bitch had been tethered and muzzled to be bred the first time, he'd felt a deep, righteous satisfaction. The animal would do what she'd been raised to do, foul tempered as she was. She'd never shown the domesticated canine desire to please, but he had nothing to prepare himself for her revenge. A part of him twinged about the pleasure he'd taken in her helpless rage, but he'd pushed the pang away. Breeding wasn't a pretty process, but it was part of the business. That night had been the first time he'd bought a bottle in what, four years? Maybe more. He'd just lost his girlfriend he'd quit drinking for, so why not?

The infrared monitor had shown the expectant dam pacing and panting the night she was due, but when he'd entered the windowless cinderblock whelping room and turned on the overhead fluorescent, he lit up a nightmare.

It was then he knew he had the tool of his vengeance. His impulse had been to destroy the bloody-mouthed miscreation then and there, surrounded by thousands of dollars' worth of her dead pups. He picked up the one that was least bloody and held it, still warm, against his chest, thinking there might be a sliver of a chance it had survived. Echoes of an earlier crime against him, committed when he was a young man full of dreams for his future, had brought another plan to his mind as he looked over the tiny, mangled bodies. The little pup cooled in the palm of his hand. Cradling it there, he'd let the wounded tears come. There was no pretending; it was gone.

*Now, at long, long last, there will be a reckoning. Free of this curse. Once and for all, free.*

He looked at his guitar in the corner, and a tune came into his head that went with those words. Every time he'd tried to play recently, he'd ended up fighting back tears and not getting into that space where the sound of his voice resonated with the strings, flowing and healing himself and anyone who heard him. Someday soon, he'd see if he could pick up a gig at the little bar he'd started visiting. He knew he was good, and he missed the feeling of an audience transfixed by his music. He could handle being around the booze now. Things were going to be better.

Now, he could get on with his life. When he'd tracked Stephanie down each time before, he'd always had to hold back. She'd done enough harm to him without him having to worry about legal consequences. She'd always talk, soothing him, pulling the resolve out of his backbone. She reminded him she was telling people about what he was doing, not that he ever did anything really. More of her lies. Now that he'd tricked her into taking in the monster, the gears of righteous process could turn without him being anywhere near.

The rage in the ghoulish bitch's glare spoke unmistakably of her loathing for humanity. If she lived, he gut-knew anyone who showed her kindness would come to regret it.

After the third time trying to get back to sleep, he gave up. He mumbled a curse to himself and got dressed. He had something to take care of before work.

# II

# PRAYER FOR HEALING

STEPHANIE LIMPED IN wearing clean scrubs she'd borrowed from Sylvie after showering in the surgery bathroom. Thin morning light washed the tiny kitchenette adjoining the surgery, catching the warm mahogany brown of Sylvie's eyes and the circles under them. Stephanie pulled up the oversized fuchsia-pink pants as she sat down. She wobbled and almost fell.

"Damn it, Steve, when you live alone, you don't eat." Sylvie chuckled and shoved a mug of coffee and a chocolate chip energy bar at her from where she sat. "When I do, I don't do anything else. Maybe if we lived together…"

She gave Stephanie a sly look, ran her fingers through the curling forelock of her graying, femininely styled buzz-cut hair and leaned back in her chair. "You promised you'd let me take you to the shrine at Sainte-Anne-de-Beaupré, back when you were first having problems with that hip. I'm gonna make you follow through on that one of these days. When your jeans come out of the dryer, I'll put that wrap on over them for you properly. You're not getting the best support out of it the way you're doing it."

Licking her chapped lips, Stephanie searched unsuccessfully for words.

"How are you dealing with life lately, anyway? You never would say much about the personal stuff, kinda like a cat hiding that it's hurt…" Sylvie kept chatting gently. "…so I'm going to play my nurse part and pry a little. You on any meds now?"

Stephanie sipped the coffee and stared at the painfully bright colors on the energy bar wrapper, unconvinced it was edible. "Gave up on the Abilify—cost me half what I make with the camp maintenance for the

From-Aways, made me feel like a zombie and didn't do shit for the anxiety or the flashbacks."

*And now I've got a bottle of useless pills instead of a new roof.*

"I hear you on the pharma." Glancing around like someone could be eavesdropping, Sylvie leaned forward. "I'm not going to tell someone they shouldn't take them—I'd appreciate the same respect out of those who say I should. Anyway, there's a secondary market for that stuff if you need to get some of your investment back. Don't say I said so, but if you should happen to accidentally leave the bottle in my purse, you could look for it there in a few days and find an envelope where you left it."

"You're risking too much for me already." Stephanie shook her head. "I don't want this to get any more one-sided than it is. I'll donate the pills if one of your clients could use them."

It wasn't entirely altruistic not to want to add to the pressures weighing on the friend who was the entirety of her support network. Thinking about what might happen if the pressure broke through was the stuff of panic attacks.

From what Stephanie had been able to piece together from their conversations and the bits of gossip she'd heard during their earlier years, Sylvie had lost at least a couple of jobs when she'd gotten so stressed the angels started talking to her. At one point the police had been called when she'd become convinced her shift supervisor, who sounded like a first-order snake, was plotting to kill her. After that incident, she'd gone into the hospital against her will on a 302 warrant. Rumors that she could become violent if she snapped had continued to follow her from employer to employer until she'd settled in Millinocket and mellowed a little.

Fluttering her fingers to shake away the idea of losing Sylvie again, Stephanie started to repeat herself, and was firmly interrupted.

"I want you to tell me you're all in on this animal, because otherwise I'm slipping a Big Sleep dose into her IV." Sylvie looked at her with hard, skeptical eyes. "I'm impressed with how you kept your shit together to help her, but now we have consequences. You'll be in on a lie to protect her, and you'll have to stick to it, anxiety or no anxiety—because if you don't, I'm going to jail. She has a wildlife tattoo, Steve. She shows up as a rescue connected to a sanctuary. You want to guess who registered it?"

Stephanie felt like she swallowed a rock. "Moonsong Refuge?"

*Fuck. He's never going to let go until he kills me. Never.*

"Yep. Jake Ferguson's signature. You're in deep here." Sylvie tapped the table with her fingertips. "Listen up. Not the time to dissociate off into your happy place. She wasn't shown as euthanized for behavioral issues like they usually do with the dams they breed illegally—she shows up as stolen. Let that percolate a bit."

"You're thinking he's setting me up?"

*So he's out here at the end of the earth, three God-forsaken miles from frozen hell. Only one reason for that.*

"It'd be a win-win-win for him. Either you turn her back over to Moonsong, you harbor an illegal animal he can call the law on you for anytime, or you're a good girl, call the game warden and have her put down."

"Yah. Win-win-win would be his style."

"We still don't know how screwed up she is. At best, the wolf in her will salivate and sneak up on rabbits in your yard while her dog part barks at them for trespassing. She's big enough to kill you or someone else if something sets her off, and she's not even full grown yet. She isn't housetrained. Never been socialized. Liability could bankrupt you. Euthanizing her would be the smart course. From what I know of him, your ex gets that'd wreck you. It might still be the best thing."

Stephanie thought about those golden eyes looking into her, and squared her shoulders. "I can't do that."

"That's why I love ya." Sylvie gave her hand a roughly affectionate rub. "I haven't submitted her records yet. I can alter the tat to a defunct husky rescue group and file accordingly."

Struggling to steady her voice, Stephanie said, "Thank you."

"Sometimes we have cosmic appointments with the two- and four-legged people that come into our lives, and the four-legs understand better about navigating those passages than we do. Just like when you brought that injured owl in here, when we didn't even know we'd both moved the same outpost of Hades. Not a lot happens by accident." Sylvie frowned. "Respect this event. In a good percentage of the world, that's not considered crazy talk—and people like us do better there—no meds, no brainwashing, no stigma." She stared into space in a way that looked unsettlingly like she was seeing something no one else could.

Stephanie nodded.

*Hold it together, Syl. You're listing pretty hard to starboard.*

"You know how hybrids bond—she's not going to let anyone else near her." Sylvie waved her hand at something out in the cosmos. "Take care of yourself so you can take care of her, because if I have to put her to sleep after all this, I'm gonna curse your ghost. I can shatter the world with a focused shout. I'm a trained Zen warrior-monk, and I will come after you in the next life if you've played me over being serious about this animal."

"I'm supposed to tell you when you're veering, Syl." Stephanie put her hand up. "Are you sure that's what you meant to say?" She didn't say "Is this the schizophrenia talking?" out loud.

"Anyway, she's spayed now." With a gesture like brushing away cobwebs from her face, Sylvie sat up straighter. "I want to be sure she doesn't develop infection in the lacerations on her forelegs that got basted in ditchwater. She's going to have a heavy limp, but at least she'll be easier to leash train. The frostbite on her ears doesn't look too terrible—those black places will leave her with a bit of serration, but her fur should hide it. She's a gorgeous beast."

Seeming like she was fully back on planet Earth, Sylvie's gaze focused steel-hard. "Her size and those yellow eyes are going to be hard to bullshit about, so don't let the game wardens see her. At least Governor Le-fucking-Page isn't being exactly vigilant on environmental regs. If there's a silver lining to his turdship, they won't be scouring the backcountry looking for violations. Anyway, I'll make sure she gets vet care, but she'll be a lot to manage, expensive to keep, and you're not exactly bringing in the big dollars—nor are you young anymore. You think on this one hard."

*Yeah, I'll probably die before she does.*

"There's something else—possible indicator of temperament." A dark expression crossed Sylvie's face. "She gave birth a couple of weeks ago, but her milk's dried up. First litter—she's maybe eight months old—too young to breed. Draw your own conclusions."

*Pups are dead. Killed them herself if she had the life I think she did.*

It was quiet for a while.

"Not that sometimes that isn't the kindest option." Folding her arms, Sylvie looked out the window. "I get the *Beloved* calculus, even if it's not one I could've made myself. One big reason why I never let any man get close to me. Chances are she didn't have a choice in the matter, unlike some of us."

The silence took on some frost.

Stephanie started fiddling with the end of her braid.

Sylvie's lips pursed in a hard line.

Stephanie mirrored the expression.

"Good-girl Catholic with your weird hypocritical Shinto hoodoo about never hurting anything. I still dream about that clinic," Stephanie finally said. "Shouldn't have listened to you then, and don't need to now. Last time, we didn't speak to each other again for a few decades."

"Buddhist. You should try it sometime. It keeps me out of the hospital and off the poisons they try to fill me with." Sylvie let out a long breath. "Some of the monks were soldiers, lethal ones. Everything's a calculation of harms, and we try to do the least damage, even when it means doing violence. You wouldn't be alive if you hadn't let me put you on that bus, never let yourself doubt it." She lowered her head. "He was going to kill you eventually if you didn't leave. A child with him would have bound you to him until the bitterest of ends. I hope you accept that now."

Stephanie clenched her teeth and stared silently at her coffee mug.

"Did you ever get any of your good things back?" Sylvie gently slid the mug aside.

"Nope. Not even my mother's pearls—I'm sure long gone, if they were real. The animals were the worst part. Still haunts me."

"What in the hell ever drew you into that evil mess, Steve?"

A towering wave of memories crashed through Stephanie's mind. A handsome man with sparkling eyes and shining teeth. The charming songs written just for her, the dogs who were more than dogs, full of a different fire. Standing with him, emptying out the liquor bottles onto the rocks at the lake, and then holding each other so tight, their tears running together as their faces pressed to each other. The wedding in the small, low-ceilinged Pentecostal church, making the vow to love, honor, and obey, because it all seemed so true and right, with Jake smiling at her in his rented tux and sun-filled grin.

"Wolf hybrids were legal when Jake hired me for the kennel. I didn't start out on the wrong side of the law—I just woke up there. Early on, was like I'd died and gone to heaven. When I moved, I thought you'd stay in touch."

*Maybe you could've come and visited me sometimes. Maybe you could've illuminated my stupidity before it got so bad you had to rescue me.*

"Yah. Love and drugs. Mind-altering potions that both go with idiocy in lockstep. That's why I never touch any of that stuff." Sylvie rolled her eyes. "I'm glad you called when you needed help. I should have gotten on that bus with you. I wanted to, but I thought I needed to stay with my work. Friends are more important."

Wiping her eye with the back of her hand, Stephanie had too many words in her mind to say any of them coherently. She swallowed hard and rubbed Sylvie's arm.

*We were married, me in my mother's necklace so she could be there with me, like we were mated for life—the animals waiting for us when we came home. I meant it then, with my whole idiot heart. I thought the wildlife refuge was so we could keep the family together after the law changed.*

*Part of that was right—it was to bind us there, but it wasn't because he thought of us as a family.*

A deep, musical yodel came from the cages in the surgery.

"Look who's awake…" Sylvie grinned at the sound. "Now, let's get your clothes out of the dryer and you can do some bonding before you go. You sure you don't want me to wrap the hip for you over the jeans? Works better that way—promise."

A flash of something uncomfortable seemed to cross Stephanie's face. A soft voice to the left and behind said, "Not to do. Not today. Not to be."

Sylvie changed the subject. "Before I forget, it dawned on me that if your ex is going to be staying around here any length of time, he's going to be working somewhere. Jobs aren't exactly popping up in the potato fields these days, so it shouldn't be too hard to check out where he might be."

"Thanks," Stephanie said. "You haven't really been around for one of these sessions yet. I didn't want you to know how bad it got to me a few years back. I thought it'd scare you off right when we were reconnecting. Was hoping he was done. As far as I know, he's stayed sober for the last few years. He brags about it every time I hear from him. Maybe it won't be too bad this time. He's getting old like the rest of us."

*If we haven't scared each other off by now...* echoed in Sylvie's head.

As soon as they opened the door, the yodeling became a crescendo of trills, wails, and gurgles. Sylvie got caught up in the joyful moment of reunion.

"She's got a great voice." Sylvie chuckled, setting aside the shadows. "Huskies don't bark, but you get a whole frickin' opera in exch— Whoa, girl! You'll wreck those fancy teeth of yours biting on stainless steel! Not even that dentition can stand up to..."

Stephanie knelt down next to the cage and cooed, "Hey, Shura, easy with that."

The dog, washed so clean her coat shimmered icy silver and white, stopped in mid gnaw. She looked Stephanie straight in the eyes through the substantial bars of the 100-150 lb. rated cage. It was as if Stephanie had spoken the name she knew herself by. Stephanie put her hand through the bars, and Shura nuzzled and pawed it with a bandaged foot, but she didn't lick. Even though she wore the cone of shame that kept her from chewing on her stitches, licking would have seemed beneath her.

Sylvie gasped. "*Oh merde...pas ce nom,*" she murmured. "Use the whole name. I was so clever I didn't think..."

Several voices wailed incoherently, behind and above.

Stephanie looked up at her. "What?"

Sylvie's pulse fluttered in her chest and neck. She tugged her Ste. Anne medal on its sturdy 10-karat chain. "It's too late." She shook her head. "She's taken the name as her crown. *Saṃsāra...Oh Ste. Anne de Beaupré, grand-mère de Dieu, protège-nous de la tempête.* Shit, I need a walk. I gotta lock this up and go. I need to turn out the lights."

Stephanie got slowly to her feet. "I'm supposed to remind you that stress causes cortisol release, and cortisol doesn't do good things for you." She wrapped her arms around Sylvie. "You need rest. You've been up all night. Let me drive you home. You shouldn't be out walking as exhausted as you are."

Sylvie pulled back. "I'll take you up on the ride, but you need to know—the diminutive should be Yuki—snow. Shura gets translated as blood, but it's fathomless deeper...the realm of the war gods...one of the six hells, eternal cycle of retribution and revenge." She put her hands on Stephanie's shoulders, her voice weary but steady. "Thanks for sticking with me, Steve. I'll shut up now."

*It's opening. The Gate. It's opening. Can't talk about it. Loose lips bring involuntary commitment forms. See the truth, be prepared, and say nothing.*

Rubbing his smooth-shaved skull, Jake wept quietly in the dark. He'd been out and back again, and still there was no daylight. The sun went down so early and came up so late. A dull orange glimmer came in the high window from the parking lot. His hands were cracked from handling frozen metal and spilled petroleum. Just looking at the guitar, thinking about the strings vibrating, made his teeth hurt. The headache was killing him, too bad to go to work.

Drone footage ran on his laptop, but there wasn't anything worth seeing. Hours of nothing. Nothing but snow and gray skies and the miserable logged-over scrubland left after the paper companies had come and gone. This desolation was a fitting place for Stephanie to have chosen to make her home. Jake felt like his heart was as barren as the landscape. The joy had been sucked out of his life.

If Stephanie hadn't left him, he wouldn't have to live like this. If she hadn't killed his baby, he could be going to a college graduation, a wedding, holding a grandchild. If she hadn't left him so messed up, he could have had another relationship that worked, and had other kids.

Instead, anyone he loved ran from him once they saw how scarred and ugly she'd left him. Every time his life was getting back on track, something would fail, and if he followed the threads to the source, it always ended up with Stephanie, Queen of the Wasteland. Sometimes he'd even go watch her for a while, let her know he was lurking so she wouldn't get too smug with thinking he'd forgotten what she did. Maybe he'd peek in on some of her mail, try to hack her accounts. Even if he never got in, at least she'd be locked out for half a day. Wasn't much satisfaction, and then she'd reach out, pull him in, talk to him and make him promise not to give her even those little reminders anymore.

*Fuck that.*

He had been doing okay, finally back on his feet, not drinking, not messing with any other chemicals either, even up to a few weeks ago when he was still living in the mobile home on the sanctuary property. It wasn't as nice as the house he'd bought with Stephanie, but it was all right. Big and newly renovated, he'd done a good job of it back then. And he'd had Bree, with her sexy little body and blonde, sometimes wildly color-streaked hair, so full of life.

Full of life...

*Stop.*

He'd held on to the house for years, but eventually he had to sell and move into the trailer. He figured Stephanie must have learned about that by now, and that she'd be laughing at him over it, but she'd left him such an emotional wreck he couldn't hold a regular job for long the way he used to. He hated to think of the satisfaction that would give her.

Then Bree had moved in with him. He'd stood with her on the banks of the little stream that ran through the sanctuary as they poured the bottles out. He thought it would be a good thing. She was a fallen person in a lot of ways, but she'd looked to him to lift her up. He tried to make it work, but he'd learned the hard way not to trust anyone. They were together for almost four years. He'd considered bringing her into the Pentecostal church, returning to it with her, but he didn't want to deal with his history in it.

He and Bree had gone to the Hands Around the Capitol rally in Augusta and seen the governor there, cheering the crowd on for defending the lives of the unborn. The tears on her windburned face at the simple, spare ceremony—the ringing of the bell and casting of the roses in the snow for each one of the babies lost that year—had seemed so genuine. Her pink, snowflake-patterned knit hat with the pompom, the color matching her cute little runny nose, the stop-sign pro-life placard tucked under her arm as she fumbled in her coat pocket for a ragged tissue. He'd stood with her, their gloved fingers interlacing shyly as they cried silently together, and he thought he'd finally found the right companion to join in his life.

The Knights of Columbus were allied with fundamentalists and Evangelicals in the cause, and their banners fluttering in the cold wind gave him an idea. He asked Bree if she wanted to join a Catholic church like he'd been raised in. She'd said that was for the French, and she wanted nothing to do with them, even if the governor did come out of that culture. She liked the picture-book pretty Congregational churches whose spires dominated the wealthy hamlets of Chamber of Commerce Maine, but they both knew those places weren't for them.

He'd laughed and agreed that French were made to stay away from, with their hard brick and stone churches high and cold on the hills, crowning their alien towns full of incomprehensible jabber. The governor had to take his college entrance tests in French because his English was so bad, but he'd risen above that, and Jake respected him for it. A man should be able to triumph over his bred-in weaknesses.

After those first good years, Jake felt things change between them. Bree was starting to give him more of an attitude. She was back to drinking, and perhaps worse. Rehab had helped for a bit, and she did go to some kind of counseling at a Baptist church that made her more womanly and gracious for a while, but it didn't seem to hold. Maybe it was just that her regular smart mouth was getting on his nerves, but he didn't like the way she sassed back instead of answering his questions. He hid a camera to make sure she wasn't cheating on him. He never did find evidence of that.

It turned out she was stealing cash from the operation. Not a lot. Just skimming. She thought she was smart, swiping passwords and tweaking records on the networked Moonsong business computer in the trailer when he was away, figuring she was safe because a good part of the operation was illegal and there was no way any cops were going to get called on her. Two could play that game. She never did figure out that he'd put a keystroke tracker on the machine. He kept screenshots of her bank transfers to show his business partner, Duke Gagnon, if he needed to, and he held on to the knowledge rather than confronting her, because things like that are useful.

When he'd found Bree had swiped the pearl necklace from the back of his sock drawer, that was different. That was private—his voodoo charm against Stephanie. Fake, just like her and her precious mother.

It wasn't hard wrapping Bree up in wire after dealing with wolf hybrids that weighed the same as she did and had bigger teeth. He even laughed when she tried to bite him. She did look cute that way, but he didn't take advantage of it. It was a point of pride, even though he liked to play with her that way when it was a game between them, and he could feel his manhood stirring as he watched her struggle. This was about justice. The necklace wasn't hard to find, since he had watched her hiding it in the couch springs.

There were things she screamed at him, and then things she said when she finally understood and started pleading for her life that made him hesitate, but he was sure it was all lies. Tape over her pretty, manipulative lips took care of that. He warned her not to cry too hard because she wouldn't be able to breathe through her mouth if her nose got runny.

After taking a couple of strong swigs of Canadian, Jake told Duke about Bree's skimming. Things weren't always smooth with him personally, but they trusted each other in the trenches, and they'd always had each other's back when third parties got nosy. Duke's wife never said a dozen words together, and was as much of a hard-ass as her husband. She could field dress a deer by herself, and she'd been even more unfriendly to fluffy little Bree than she was to most people. She wasn't likely to go searching out what might have happened if the precious twat became scarce at the compound.

Jake sniffled and wiped his eyes a lot while he showed Duke where she'd fucked around in the company books and then told him that he had her back at the trailer. Duke took care of things from there. Bree had been the type of girl whose friends and family wouldn't be surprised if she went off the radar for a while, and would believe it when they were told she'd come and gone again. It was true she'd left for some unknown destination, one from which no traveler returns.

There was a huge wood-fired kiln on the property. Duke's wife Sarah was a potter who sold her stuff at craft fairs. Sanctuary Vessels, out of Moonsong Refuge. Had a nice ring to it, and the wild-animal-patterned raku mugs and bowls sold well. The fire had to be kept going, could take a week to get it up to temperature if it cooled down. Sometimes a euthanized animal went into the flames when there were no visitors around. It was quick and sanitary.

Duke told him not to worry, that everything was taken care of. That was weeks ago now, time to let it go.

After that, Jake felt like he had to move out. Get on the road. Do something different. Stephanie had marked him, cursed him for so long, making everything in his life fail. Making him kill Bree for stealing the damned cheap-ass imitation pearls was the worst thing yet.

He didn't really kill her, he wasn't the one who did, never even seeing how she'd been…

*Stop.*

Bree must have thought the junk beads were real to risk it, sucked in by the lies that clung to everything Stephanie touched.

Time to clear that curse, once and for all. No more half measures. The machinery was in motion. All those times she went witchy on him, making his guts feel like they were full of cold water. The times she cooed and hummed to the animals in that weird, soft, spooky voice and made them roll over and show her their bellies. That trick would go south on her real fast once she saw what his gift to her was made of.

She wouldn't have that evil power over him or anyone else, soon enough. No more sweet talk, bending his brain into pretzels. She and that crazy friend he could never get her all the way away from, that one who kept turning up like a hex after years of being gone. Poisoning her mind. That "friend."

He reminded himself to do a close drone flight around the veterinary office when he felt better.

Tired as she was, Sylvie still carefully polished each of the shelf-sized metal statues populating her shrine as she played whatever music worked with where she needed her focus to be. Her go-to was usually her Leonard Cohen playlist, but this time she chose chants from a Tibetan monastery. The polishing to music was a vital part of her daily ritual. Time blurred in her mind, unclear whether it was the morning or evening devotion she was practicing, but neglecting her sacred objects would invite savagery and chaos. She spent extra time with a pair of ferocious six-inch copper divinities accented with polished brass and tiny chips of red crystals, long-fanged adolescent girls adorned with severed heads and a variety of weapons.

These were the gentler aspects of dakini manifestation. Others, ones she didn't keep statues of on her deep-blue-satin-covered table, had the bodies of hags and the heads of animals. Tibetan Buddhism raised the devotion to dark energy to a higher level than any she'd seen outside the viciously authoritarian convent school where she'd been boarded as a child.

The exile from her home had been for Sylvie's safety, because her mother had fought similar battles with her own brain, and turned to religion for refuge the same way. She entrusted the nuns to care for her daughter when the storms grew too wild. There had been good, kind nuns there as well as monsters, but they'd had to fight against the currents to offer what protection they could.

Like Sylvie, her mother danced between what her world designated as the polar opposites "sacred" and "profane." Mme Antoine-Labbot prided herself on her abilities as a fortune teller, despite swearing that cartomancy and palmistry were tools of the Devil. She warned her daughter that if she were to take them up, she would condemn herself to eternal damnation.

Sylvie came by the heritage fully, but before her mind had even begun spinning widdershins on her as a welcome to adulthood, she'd had enough nightmares about cannibalistic holy women stalking graveyards to last her a lifetime. She left the wrathful aspects of the dakinis to devotees who could better accommodate the worship of them..

The youthful divinities, with their dainty vampire mouths, drinking blood from skull cups, their lithe multi-armed bodies flourishing skinning knives, daggers, and flower-covered but lethal arrows, were harrowing enough. Their force was essential to Sylvie's balancing act though, and she treasured them even as she wished she could access their blessings more respectfully.

*Vajrayogini, Kurukullā, forgive me for not knowing your proper mantras. I have been searching for the right mantra…I don't know Sanskrit…I try to find the true words…Forgive me for never learning your language, forgive me for my ignorance I pray you, and accept my devotion. I turn to you to teach me the right and noble energy converging…*

Sometimes the figures spoke to her, but in that moment there was only silence. Quiet was usually a mercy, but now she listened hopefully. The only answer was no answer. Male Kuan Yin on his Heart Sutra-inscribed moon smiled calmly. Kuan Yin, the one who hears the wounded cries of the world, the bodhisattva of compassion who won't adhere to a fixed gender and hears voices.

Turning to the two-inch miniature of Kuan Yin in female form, riding the waves while standing serenely on a dragon's back, she thought of the Blessed Sainte Anne, Mother of Mary, another protector of seafarers and those who struggle in the tide. The Ste. Anne medal the kindest nun, her namesake, had given her for her First Communion felt like a warm glow over her heart.

Sister Mary Anne had been there to pick up dozens of those minor dropped stitches of life after her mother was released from the hospital. From her, Sylvie had learned to love the Grandmother of God, and entrust her with her prayers. The sister had been at her First Communion with her cheap camera and sweet smile while Sylvie's mother nodded in the front pew, too heavily drugged to remember the ceremony afterward.

Sister Anne's letters and the photographs she'd taken of Sylvie in her little girl's version of a wedding gown and veil were tucked carefully in a box in her bedroom. They never seemed to belong in the shrine room; they were personal, full of friendship and kindness that had lasted until the nun had passed away not long before Sylvie moved to Millinocket.

She decided to set her timer to allow an extra ten minutes for her meditation session and after that to repeat the morning's novena in case she hadn't actually said it, but was only remembering the intent.

The large color photograph at the left side of the shrine, set level with the thangka of Vajradhara Buddha on the right, at the highest point of any sacred image in her house, caught her eye and held it. The beautiful, thin-faced woman, elderly and magnificent, raised her blonde little daughter in star-robed glory. The heavy gilded plaster crowns, the red and golden paint...

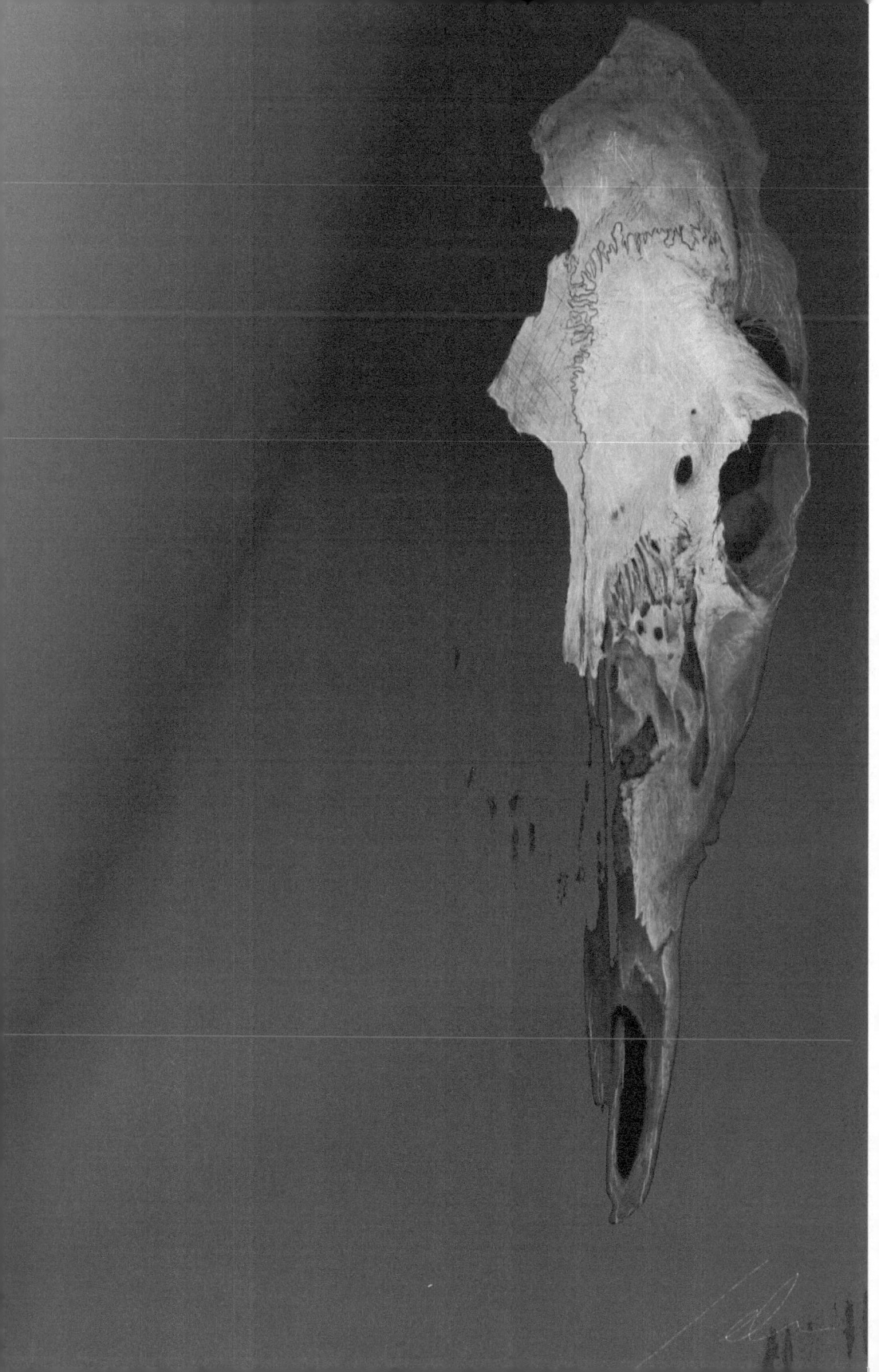

# III

# PRAYER FOR PROTECTION

STEPHANIE TOOK THE long way home, alone in the small hours on the Golden Road. The wrap around her hip was indeed more supportive and more comfortable. It might be a trick to get free of it in time to pee when she got in, but for the protracted time at the wheel, it was a help.

The Golden was an easier drive, she had to admit, and it probably took about the same amount of time even though the miles were longer. It seemed like she didn't have to squint and rub her eyes as much. The headlights didn't play with the shadows in the trees the same way they did on the shortcut, and she thought to herself maybe she should only take the fire access in daylight.

Yellow eyes still stalked Jake all through his late morning headache sleep. Something about the prow of a ship. A storm.

Bree's voice, pleading for her life…pleading for two lives…

He forced himself awake, trembling, and took a handful of pills that sent him into a dreamless void.

Stephanie hadn't bothered to try to sleep when she'd got in after driving Sylvie home. The hour or two of rest weren't worth the effort. She was done at the Twin Lakes camp after photographing the water running so the owners would know the lines hadn't frozen, a light burning to show the power was on, and the gauge on the bottled gas. She'd just sent the time-stamped pics. She had made it through her morning rounds in a caffeinated trance, then stopped for her regular sandwich in town. The cabins past the Baptist church were her last of the day, and she was relieved to be finally heading home under the blessing of clear daylight. Repeating to herself "Take the Golden," she rehearsed the unfamiliar route so she wouldn't revert to old habit.

She avoided looking as she drove past the church on her way back to the main road. The movable-lettered sandwich-board sign stuck out of the plowed-snow ridge along the roadside, admonishing her that every abortion stops a beating heart.

The tiny thing she'd had removed from her belly no doubt still had a tail, but its heart surely pulsed translucent red through itself. It had pulled nourishment out of her body to grow according to its inexorable blueprint. The fusion of Jake with her flesh had never felt like it belonged there. Another life inside hers, becoming. The clinic had invited her to counselling after the procedure, but she'd turned it down. She had to get moving before her crime was discovered. The biological imperative was an alien process, something she had no instinct for. It was just the cruelty she'd regretted, ugly tears running down her face as she got on the bus headed for the turnpike.

Sylvie's decades-gone words echoed, asking if it was really the grief of loss she felt, or just guilt for the crime of putting herself first.

Sometimes in her dreams the thing flopped after her, big as a toddler, needing to feed. She knew its bulbous eyes, hidden behind fused skin, were Jake's sparkling blue. It would curl and writhe like a worm on a summer rock, mewling in pain. She'd stand frozen, staring at it, knowing it would attach itself like a lamprey if she let it get near enough. There was never a resolution.

Blinking hard, she put the thought aside.

Her phone pinged a notice that Sylvie had texted her. At the intersection, she pulled off to the side of the road, her hazard lights flashing.

*Hey. Been doing some circumspect/discreet checking & heard J was doing heating oil deliveries. Word is he's got a year's lease on an apt. Gotta go. Lock up even tighter.*

An urgent impulse to get home vetoed the idea of going the long way around on the Golden. It was the middle of a sunny day, after all.

Turning left instead of right, and then taking the fire road, Stephanie twinged with a late surge of caution. Something compelled her to pull off at the same spot as the night before, almost believing that none of it had been real. It wouldn't have surprised her to see the snow undisturbed, confirming that life was still what passed for normal. She wasn't clear on why, but something tugged at her, making her belly twinge. It felt like a century had passed, but it had been less than eighteen hours since she'd rescued Shura from the ditch.

The midday sun sparkled on fresh, blowing powder. Several vehicles had passed since she was there last, their tracks softened by the overnight snowfall and stiff morning wind. A cluster of crows hopped and squabbled, perhaps attracted by Shura's blood. The depression in the snowbank where she'd been lying seemed bigger than it had the night before. Stephanie wiped her glasses on her scarf.

Then she saw the wire. Reminded by the tangible thing, she clearly remembered throwing it into the ditch so it wouldn't tangle in someone's wheel. Now the twisted copper was sticking up in the drift, planted like a flagpole. The crows worried at something near the base of it.

Stephanie grabbed her phone. The connection crackled but went through. "Sylvie here. Very sorry…call you back. I…assisting Doctor…surgery."

Stephanie lifted the rifle off the rack and put a round in the chamber. It was only a .22, but she was a decent shot with it when she wasn't shaking. She tried to work on that part.

She hardly felt her feet touch the ground as she approached the crows. They burst up and cursed from the birch and evergreen branches overhead.

The thing they'd been fighting over was mostly red, about the size of a baby rabbit. Its fur, what was left of it, was pure, shimmering white. Something was wrapped several times around its torn throat. Stephanie touched her own neck, looking at it.

*Pearls.*

After sending the text about Jake to Stephanie, Sylvie activated the in-surgery phone message so she could attend to herself. She needed to perform her practice, and it had gotten knocked off track by all the animal drama.

The focus of her Buddhist observation had made a great wandering from its roots grown in the soil of Himalayan mythology through ancient Warring States Chinese Taoism to the refined savagery of Imperial Japan and back again. As she dug deeper for the vein of understanding, the search kept her located in her own brand of sanity.

She'd found her centerpoint after throwing herself at white wall Zen, immersed in the study of Samurai koans from the harsh temples of Kamakura. Stare at the wall and sit. Just sit. Think of nothing. Nothing. That's it. No ceremonial liturgy but a few short sutras and a hundred brain-breaking koans. No special mantras to memorize phonetically. The warriors were illiterate and used to battle, without patience for rituals; they were assigned a common-language koan of a few paragraphs designed to be a personalized purgatory. The priests met their obtuseness with blows from their long staffs. All of them practiced to prepare for death.

Sylvie had stared at the wall until something happened. Something small, startling, and familiar from her readings in gentler teachings. Tibetan descriptions of the art of meditation described the appearance of the "pearl" when the mind was sufficiently quiet, and the glowing point hovering before her unfocused eyes could meet that description. In the pearl was healing. In the pearl was calm, *mens sana*, acceptance of things.

Pulling herself stiffly into a half-lotus, Sylvie began a chant of the Heart Sutra.

*Avalokita, the Holy Lord and Bodhisattva, was moving in the deep course of the Wisdom which has gone beyond.*

*He looked down from on high, He beheld but five heaps, and He saw that in their own-being they were empty.*

The five skandas—aggregates, heaps of clinging and craving: impression of form, sensation of the material, perception, concepts, consciousness. Sylvie had no problem grappling with the idea. Hallucinations had been her regular companions since her late teens—she just had more of them and they were more dissonant than the ones most people lived with.

She reminded herself to stay with her breathing.

*There is no decay and death, no extinction of decay and death. There is no suffering, no origination, no stopping, no path.*

Pain and fear. Just one and one more gift from the brain that keeps on giving. Setting her timer for half an hour, Sylvie looked at the plain wall until her breaths came slow and shallow, and then the glow appeared, washing her fevered synapses with quiet.

And more quiet.

Startled by the alarm, she stretched her numb legs in front of her and rubbed them for a few minutes before attempting to turn around and kneel.

Then the third prayer of her novena, delivered toward the photograph from the Basilica at Beaupré.

*Glorious Ste. Anne, filled with compassion for those who invoke thee and with love for those who suffer, heavily laden with the weight of my troubles, I cast myself at thy feet...*

She repeated the prayer three times.

*Remember, O glorious and Good Ste. Anne, Mother of the Queen of Heaven, that never was it known that anyone who fled to thy protection...*

When she turned her phone back on, there were seven messages from Stephanie.

# IV

# PRAYER FOR MERCY

THE PILLS WERE wearing off. Jake took a couple of long pulls from his flask.

*Need to let up on this soon, buddy. Today's not the day, but this ain't good.*

He'd awakened several times in a cold sweat, his mind churning. The self-medication fucked with his sleep patterns, giving him straitjacket night terrors, the recollection of which he had to block out if he wanted to try closing his eyes again. Finally falling asleep for a couple of hours steady, he woke up with blessed, if foul-tasting, amnesia.

Checking the time on his muted phone, he realized he'd missed the chance to do a flyover of his latest tableau before Stephanie had most likely found it. Shreds of memories floated by, and he grabbed at them.

He jolted to fully awake. What if Duke hadn't gone through with it? What if he'd softened to see Bree there like that? Duke Gagnon was as cold-blooded as he needed to be, but there had been times he'd shut Jake's ramblings down when they ran to particular tastes. Jake had kept to himself what he did with the bitch he'd left for Stephanie to find, just saying he'd dealt with the animal because she was too savage to breed. They'd agreed she was too much of a liability, and that was where they'd left it.

A sleep-paralysis episode from a few hours before buzzed into Jake's head. As he'd lain there unable to move, Bree had stumbled into the room, her belly swollen and her hair full of ashes from the kiln. She'd wailed and squatted, and something had been born from her, something premature with closed, bulbous eyes and savage teeth that tore her body as it emerged, carried in an amniotic fluid of ditchwater and blood.

Jake grabbed for his phone as the dream came into focus. He'd avoided considering the obvious, and that could possibly bite hard. Too much drinking, not enough thinking—or too much thinking about the wrong things. Fingers shaking, it took him a couple of tries to open the app to access the records of the motion-activated camera in the trailer. He should have pulled it down, should have got it out of there, but if it was still in place, that meant no one knew it was watching. It would show what had happened a few weeks ago, so long as there wasn't enough movement in the meantime to use up the storage space.

Scrolling through the still shots of the unchanged room every six hours, he watched the days and nights flicker by. Clenching the phone, he muttered "C'mon, c'mon," and worried the memory cache had dumped the critical moments almost as much as he dreaded that they were still there. He didn't need to be concerned about the capacity. There was abundant time stretching backward, rivers of soundless, speeded-up low-res monochrome video from Bree's final hours, and before, from their fights and their ordinary habits dancing by in reverse as he shot too far into the past.

After hitting the end of the feed, he advanced again at half the rate. There was Bree, pleading, struggling, then helpless. Slowing to real time, he watched the two hours pass, the feed stopping and lurching forward because she lay so still.

Then Duke entered the trailer. Jake was no lipreader, but he appeared to apologize as he knelt next to Bree and laid a dark plastic bag over her face, pinning her head down firmly. Her eyes had opened wide before they were hidden, and she thrashed briefly as Duke pressed what someone who didn't know might have thought was the end of a nightstick against her forehead. There were perhaps a half-dozen bolt stunners around the sanctuary, used to humanely dispatch animals.

Flinching at the silent concussion, Jake put his hand to his mouth. When Duke pulled the tool away, he laid it on a rag that picked up a dark smear, and reached into his jacket for a long, thin strip of plastic. Jake gagged but forced himself to keep watching. Duke carefully slid the tip of the pithing rod into the small hole in the plastic. The form underneath stayed motionless.

Jake heaved and sobbed.

Jolting as his phone dinged, he dropped it. There was a text from his boss.

*Sorry*, he wrote back. *Gotta puke. Get back to you tomorrow.*

Sylvie held Stephanie while she shook. She brushed the wet hair off Stephanie's face where it had stuck in her tears.

Stephanie's mind floated in an abyss.

"I can't..." she said, "...not after seeing that. I can't take them."

"They are *Śarīra*." Sylvie's words had a glint of stress fracture in them, like the angels were breaking through. "Shari pearls from the ashes of the dead. The essence that survives the fire. You can't insult—"

Stephanie shook her head. Her friend was losing it. This had to stop.

"Steve... I took care of it." Sylvie's voice was steadier. "I'm going to send the poor little pup to be cremated. He probably never even drew a breath in this world. His eyes would never open. He didn't have to learn the life she'd been condemned to. Mama severed his spine at the neck, likely before he knew what happened. She was the best mother she could be in hell."

Feeling the jagged sobs taking over again, Stephanie tried to form thoughts and make words out of them. Sylvie hushed her.

"The little body was frozen solid, no contamination to be concerned about. I washed everything up. When it comes back, I'll bury the box in the clinic plot." Sylvie reached into her purse. "These are yours. I washed them and then rinsed them in Holy Water. I asked Ste. Anne de Beaupré to bless them, and she revealed herself to me. The Mother of the Blessed Mother wants you to have this connection. She told me you are in danger, and she will protect you. She appeared like a shimmer of sea-spray emerging from the torrent, as she always does in a true vision."

Holding Sylvie's arm, Stephanie fumbled a question about whether she was feeling okay.

"I'm fine." Sylvie gently freed herself. "Just respect the sign, or it could come back to bite you—you and me both, since I was the one who asked her for help. Mary was an only child, born late, like you. These are your link to the Grandmother of God. Jake never sold them, because he knew their power. Now he's tried to use them against you, but you have them back. Pearls are *lachryma*, Steve...these are your mother's sacred tears."

She pressed the necklace into Stephanie's hand.

Stephanie closed her fingers around them.

Sylvie lit a votive to Ste. Anne and prepared herself for her evening meditation. There were times she wished she'd taken one of the orphans that were regularly delivered to the veterinary clinic, but was grateful she hadn't given in to the temptation. She'd always managed to place them so as not to have to deal with the needs of another sentient being dependent on her. There would be no fur-person interrupting her concentration tonight.

Dakini Vajrayogini's slim body sang and shimmered with energy, and her polished brass fangs glinted with seductive fury. The bronze ghanta bell was calling her. The Sanskrit inscription chanted as its words crawled around the rim, living and vibrant, and when she rang it, the sound penetrated through space so that her being became fused with the dimensions beyond the skandhas.

It had been a long, bleak day, mostly spent in bed, twice throwing up from the headache and the void that howled behind it. Jake was walking down a long, shadowy corridor. Earlier, he'd done something he couldn't quite remember that had made him feel good, something to Stephanie, but now, thinking about it even around the edges made him feel nauseous again. Stephanie always ended up making him feel that way, but when he thought about what to do to fix the problem, it made him even sicker. There was something else, too—something he really needed to do, but he couldn't bring it to mind.

He was vaguely aware he was asleep, and that he wanted not to be.

There was a dark shape at the end of the hall, like a pyramid with rounded edges. As he got closer, he saw it was resting on a low, wide pedestal. He didn't want to see it any more clearly.

The thing was mumbling and chanting, and Jake fought to pull himself awake. Then he saw that it was Stephanie's weird fat friend with her nasty crewcut, dressed in black robes like some kind of Oriental monk, sitting cross-legged with the soles of her feet pointing up the way they did. She looked harmless, so deep in her nonsense she looked like she was in a drugged stupor, fingering her prayer beads. He laughed at his own fear.

She opened her eyes. They were yellow, and the shimmering white beads were smeared with red. As she counted her prayers, blood trickled from between her fingers. He thrashed himself into semi-consciousness as she began to smile. He knew what her teeth would look like.

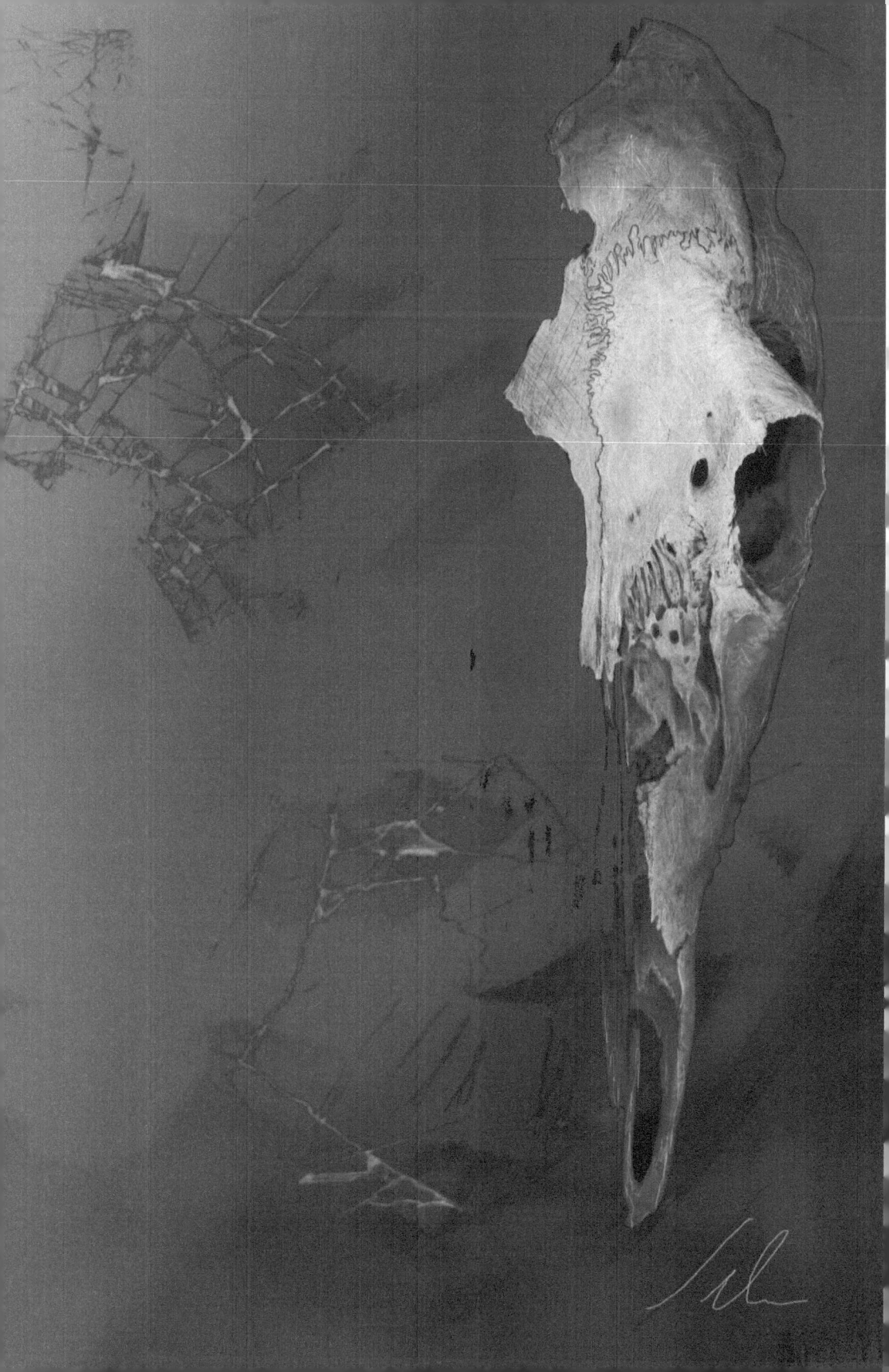

# V

# PRAYER OF INVOCATION

STEPHANIE SET THE landline ringer to its loudest and inched up the cursed ladder to the sleeping loft where the heat settled overnight. Down below, she'd left the taps and shower nozzle dripping so the pipes wouldn't freeze and burst. The fumes from the kerosene heater were nasty in the loft, but she didn't have the stamina to fill the woodstove enough to last until morning.

When she'd bought the cabin a half-decade before, it had felt like an adventure. Lately, it was a sentence in Purgatory. She hadn't fired up the furnace since she'd bought the place. Using a woodstove had made her feel resourceful and independent. Now, even feeding a pellet stove would probably be more physically demanding than she might be able to handle in a few years.

She'd made the move after the fourth time Jake had gotten re-fixated on her after something had gone wrong in his life. Everything was her fault when his world would go sideways, as it seemed inevitably to do at least two or three times a decade. He'd start harassing her in stupid little ways, just enough to unbury her PTSD symptoms but not enough to get himself in trouble. Underestimating the depth of his spite, Stephanie had thought she'd be too unimportant to follow when she'd moved away from the part of the state they'd lived in together.

When she'd found an injured owl and brought it to the vet in her adopted town around the time of the last bout of Jake's stalking, she'd reconnected with one of the few friends she'd had from before she was married. It had made her think for a moment that she could have a life of her own there in her tiny, outdated A-frame cabin in a cluster where half the camps weren't kept up anymore, sheltering more raccoons than vacationers.

She'd been bold enough to brag about it in a letter without a return address she'd sent to Jake in response to his bothering her father at the nursing home. That was one more point where she'd played the wrong card. Of course Jake tracked her down from the clues she'd let slip, and that had turned into the last round of niggling torments that ended soon after she re-met Sylvie.

Fortunately for her, Jake had found a new source of amusement, and abruptly stopped the vague, disturbing notes in her mailbox and roadkill tableaux at the foot of her driveway. His last note said he'd found the love of his life and he'd never stoop to bother with her again. That was the unnervingly syncopated rhythm of Stephanie's world, anxiously waiting for the next time, wondering how bad it would be, and then dissociating into numbness when it came.

She'd dutifully documented the incidents and forwarded them to the disinterested sheriff on Sylvie's advice, but nothing came of it. Jake had pulled his punches just enough that they could be labeled pranks. No one but Stephanie and Sylvie seemed to think the intermittent stalking could escalate into anything more, and forcing the point was likely to be counterproductive.

Now Jake was back. Shura's wounds said he was at another level of dangerous this time. The storm loomed ugly and dark, and Stephanie's boat had been taking on water for a while.

*Sylvie's right. How the hell am I going to handle an untrained 120-pound adolescent beast more than half timber wolf? Who am I kidding?*

The late afternoon sun made the loft too warm, and full of heavy amber light. Stephanie pulled the quilt over her head and fell into a mineshaft of exhausted sleep.

*The yellow glare had ebbed to a sickly glow, and the heat was oppressive. Stephanie couldn't move. Something was cutting into her wrists—copper wire. A dull wave of panic became a throb as she saw what she dreaded crouching at the foot of her bed.*

*Jake held up an oil-soaked rag twisted into an obscene shape. "You getting all dried up down there, Stephie. This should get ya warmed up."*

*He held a lighter near the rag, then set it aside and started pulling her ankles apart.*

*There is a deadly shout that Zen-trained warriors make, that comes from below the hells of Saṃsāra to pry open the dimensions and shatter the material world. She brought it up from there, made in the form of "Shura!"*

*Everything was ringing noise and howling gods.*

Sylvie woke up to the ghanta ringing, many ghantas ringing. The song was like a thousand icicles thawing and shattering. As she stood from the chair she'd fallen asleep in, the floor seemed to flush away with a surge of watery, translucent knives, the clear slush cutting into her ankles. They felt like she'd been sitting deep in meditation and the circulation was impeded. She took a long, steady breath, and the effect subsided.

The ringing was softer, and distant. Stepping cautiously, she kept verifying one sense with another, touching the dry floor, covering her ears and then releasing them. The sound was probably in her head. There were no ice floods pouring into her house. Her body surged with tremors that were probably fear, self-made in and of her own brain. Usually the hallucinations were more or less companionable, but sometimes they turned savage. Cold terror threatened to submerge her.

Glowing ice crept from under the door of the guest bedroom she used for her shrine, and the bells sang from inside. Backing into the living room, Sylvie unlocked her phone and pulled up the psychiatrist's emergency number. She'd done this a half-dozen times before; each time she'd felt she was becoming unbalanced enough to be forced to use it, and each time she'd overcome the shattering and left the number uncalled. The hospital was a known fear, and nothing she'd seen yet was worth making that choice.

The luminous glow crawled down the hall toward her. Just then, she wished she had some other creature in the house to verify the external reality of her perceptions. A black tomcat started to materialize by the door, and she let out a yelp of frustration. The cat disappeared and the glow receded under the gap at the threshold.

*Good. Good. Pull it together, Syl. This always happens when you're trying to tell yourself something you don't want to know. You're awake-dreaming again, and this is just a nightmare. You have a crossed circuit in your brain—remember remember remember that.*

*Your dreams crawl down the wires into your wakes and your thoughts get reflected on the outside surfaces and bounce back at you like they belong to someone else. But. They. Don't. They're all yours. You need to make peace with whatever it is, or it's going to keep harassing you. Paranoid psychotic breaks and nightmares don't come out of nothing. You've learned that the hard way.*

Then the voices started in. As they usually did, they seemed to come from beside, behind, and above her, the familiar personas all yammering in a discordant chorus, some calling her a coward, urging her to go forward into whatever it was, and some whimpering and wailing for her not to, to call the doctor, to stay safe.

Then one, clear, loud, ungendered, from directly in front of her, in the room, said, "Put the phone down and open the fucking door, Sylvie."

She did.

The room was staggeringly brilliant, full of moonlight spangled with swirling snow crystals.

The photograph of Ste. Anne de Beaupré opened into the towering arched ceiling of her chapel, the glided rays surrounding her struggling to come to radiant life. In Sylvie's mind, the beautiful old woman had become intertwined with Stephanie from the moment she'd come into Darrow Veterinary Clinic with the owl. Stephanie's skin had aged clear and she'd stayed slim, with that wonderous detachment. Underneath the statue's cowl, Sylvie could imagine the thick, gray braid.

The plaster Ste. Anne raised her crowned baby, gloriously robed in the colors of the vaulted sky—celestial blue spangled with shimmering stars. The statue looked at her and smiled, long-fanged and grinning. It sank its teeth into the back of the neck of the painted child, and then stared at Sylvie with raw ferocity.

"You wanted to know your mantra, here it is. This. Now."

Shura looked through the bars of her tiny den. She was alone and uncomfortable, but she felt safe. The Rescuer and the Healer would keep watch, as she would do for them.

She'd been traveling in her dreams, and they were good dreams, full of sweet blood. Her body knew it would never run like that again in the hard world of the senses, and that though the chains were gone, she'd never get to feel the hunt that called from her veins. Not in this incarnation. Sighing, she adjusted the curl of her spine and returned to the running space.

As she did, a new dream flooded her from outside, full of her name, and she bared her teeth in her sleep.

Sylvie's voice was barely audible over Shura's yowls through the answering machine. "Your she-monster needs to go home *soon*, Steve. She's in back with the door closed—I'm in the waiting room and I can't hear myself think. I can't open up the clinic with this going on."

Stephanie called the office number. Even though she sounded rougher than usual when she picked up, Sylvie asked gently about how she was feeling. The tender undertone was unexpected.

Trying to speak, and trying again, Stephanie managed to force out, "Nightmare. Need a minute."

Sylvie muttered something like "Been there, done that," before the sound of the receiver being set smartly on the counter.

Stephanie gulped down a glass of water. When she picked up the phone, Sylvie was talking in the background and Shura was wailing more softly, like a toddler whose meltdown has subsided into sobs.

Sylvie asked Stephanie to talk to her damned beast through the phone.

She cleared her throat. "Hey, lady, did you miss me?"

Shura was quiet, and then made a clear, articulate, modulated growling statement. The sulfur started clearing from Stephanie's head.

Sylvie got back on the line. "So, Steve. How are we holding up?"

Stephanie took in a deep breath. "Syl, I think I was traveling in your world last night. I know you say Zen is the map and Saint Anne is the guide, and we get messages in code from the universe, and I'm almost ready to agree with that. I need to think some things through with you. He's going to kill me this time, if he can. I know it in my bones. I feel like I'm in an old fairytale, but there's always some different spin on it every time it's acted out. I'll come visit with her tonight, and we can talk."

Sylvie said, "Yah. I think we need to do that. You don't sound so good."

Dr. Marcus Darrow called out a goodbye from the hall door to the waiting room. Sylvie listened for the old man's footsteps, and then the tinkle of the brass bell that had announced the opening and shutting of the clinic door since long before she'd worked there.

As the tinkle subsided, Sylvie shook off the sense that he'd stepped out into a void that surrounded the clinic. Reminding herself to breathe slowly and concentrate on the movement of air in and out of her body, she fought the pull of panic. Her pulse hammered. The veins on her hands wanted to coil and writhe, crawling serpent-like toward her heart, full of venom and fear. The teeth of the Madonna's mother…

Stephanie's thin, brittle arms around her had been an anchor, and now Sylvie wondered if it had been a good idea to try to open her eyes to the illusions of the world. If Stephanie was losing her grounding, then there'd be nothing keeping both of them from flying out into the emptiness.

She'd retreated from the worn Formica reception desk into the kitchenette because the printed dark oak grain under her computer had begun to heave and twist. The cords now tangled and stretched from around the far side of the doorway, preventing the door from closing. The arrangement couldn't continue during business hours, but it had to be what it was.

When Darrow had asked if she was feeling well, she'd told him she had a headache, which was true enough, but she generally worked through her headaches. He let her handle things in her own manner. The work always got done, even when the storms of angels battered her. The veterinary clinic job was the longest she'd ever held, nearly ten years, and she wouldn't let it slip away.

Losing herself in her work, she completed the updates to patient files. Then she made a couple of phone calls to owners whose bewildered animals shared the row of surgery cages with blessedly silent Shura. When she was done with that, she carried the computer and office phone back out to the reception area.

A few whimpers from the aging beagle recovering from surgery for a badly infected sebaceous cyst pointed up the deep silence. He shuffled and resettled himself with a pained sigh, and then the quiet closed in like a chloroformed rag.

Going back to the search she'd begun on her lunch break, Sylvie pulled up the tabs on the background check service she used to watch for any bad news about herself that might come up. So far, the two-decade-old police report from Vermont had stayed buried, and the psychiatrist had honored his promise to keep her involuntary commitment confidential if she stayed out of trouble. Her inpatient stay was simply described as "occupational therapy" for "extreme fatigue/exhaustion disorder." Exhaustion disorder was a newfangled term when the psychiatrist had used it, but he was correct in saying it would have a better ring to future employers than other ways he might have described her condition.

Breanna Carlton had the same legal address as Jacob Ferguson, going back several years, according to the service. A little woman, primped for her driver's license photo with freshly bleached-blonde hair and a sad, painted smile. The monthly fee Sylvie paid, about the price of a nice meal, got her access to collected records she could have found eventually on her own, but the convenience was worth it to her. Digging into the lives of random strangers and other subjects of interest was a minor vice she allowed herself. She got the benefits of gossip without risking the exposure.

The driver's license, an expired beautician's permit, and an eviction notice were all Sylvie could find from before Breanna had shared the address, shown on tax records as a mobile home on a lot owned by Moonsong. Only a speeding ticket and a citation for public intoxication, later dismissed on condition of her attending drug counselling sessions once a week, were evidence of her more recent existence. The identification picture for the rehab clinic showed dark roots, thickly applied makeup, and an even sadder, but determined, smile.

Probate notices from several weeks ago in the Portland Press Herald and Lewiston Sun Journal indicated Breanna as the beneficiary named in the will of someone who appeared to be her brother. More searching showed the estate had just been closed with the personal items unclaimed and the small cash account going to the main creditor, an inpatient substance abuse facility. She called the most recent cell number for Breanna. It didn't ring, only making a weird electronic wail in response to the call.

Wiping the corner of her eye and clearing a tightness in her throat, Sylvie searched for another phone number.

The voice that picked up carried the heavy regional French accent she expected. "Allo, Moonsong, Leduc Gagnon speaking."

Channeling the bureaucratic inflection she'd come to know too well, Sylvie said, "Good afternoon, Mr. Gagnon, this is Cassandra Letourneau, MSW with New Horizons Behavioral Health. I'm sorry to trouble you, but the contact number I have for Ms. Breanna Carlton seems no longer to be in service, and I'm newly assigned to her case. I have you listed as her landlord. Is that correct?"

There was mumbling at the other end.

"Ya, I 'ave to warn you, if you can't get her to talk to me, an' you don't know where she is, afraid we need to do a welfare visit…" Sylvie went with her instinct, reaching out as a comradely fellow frog, subject of even greater prejudice since the unpopular governor had stirred up old ethnic and religious animosities. "This girl, she had marks on her last time she came in—maybe some she did herself, some not possible. Now she's missed three sessions and no call. We gotta check. Sorry. Gonna give you a day or so, all I can do, before we notify the sheriff. Not my place to give advice—but you need to take care who you let to live in your place, okay?"

The voice on the other end radiated tension as it gave a quick thanks and hung up.

Sylvie took her mother's Grimaud *Tarot de Marseille* deck from her purse, where she'd kept it to shuffle every time she'd felt the impulse through the day. She removed it from the tin box and shuffled it once more, pulled three cards and laid them out on the kitchenette table. Past, present, future. She'd done it more than a dozen times in the last hour since the clinic closed, and the cards still made no sense. The King of Swords reversed kept coming up in different positions, along with the Queen, usually upright. That was maybe understandable. Steve was a good fit for *la reine d'épée* even if she wouldn't see herself that way. The third card would never repeat, so there wasn't a rhythm to read.

Trying another tack, Sylvie took the card she'd long used to represent herself, pulling it out and reading the energy from cards on either side. *La force*, the woman overpowering a leonine monster by gripping its jaws, kept slipping from her hands when she attempted to cut it into the deck to see where it would choose to be. The card had jammed against a bad one, *la maison Dieu*, the Tower, and then it was too spiky to hold onto.

Taking in a deep breath, she willed herself to ride the currents in her mind rather than fighting against them. She closed her eyes, re-envisioning the Grandmother floating serenely above the torrent, and supported the deck loosely in her right hand to repeat the cut. She held the Strength card at arm's length, her fingers trembling from all the spiky things coming out of it, and pleaded with it.

*Please, Ste. Anne, show me what I have to do.*

The silence rang. Then it tolled.

"This. Now."

The spikes hurt her fingertips so much she dropped the deck. It fell mostly face down, scattered across the linoleum floor.

# VI

# PRAYER FOR THE DEPARTED

JAKE ACHED, THINKING of Bree's pretty body, and the things she used to do for him, things he'd only gotten any other woman to do by paying for it. Things Stephanie should have done, since she was his wife. He should have met Bree first. That way he could have reached her and made her not do those things. Bree would have been a better partner to him if he hadn't been so damaged by his marriage.

Wound in wire, her teeth…

*No. Go away.*

He heaved a sigh that felt like it came up from the soles of his feet.

*Father of all, we pray to you for Bree, and for all those whom we love but see no longer. Grant to them eternal rest. Let light perpetual shine upon them. May her soul and the souls of all the departed, through the mercy of God, rest in peace.*

Fumbling for flap on the votive box, Jake's hand shook.

*Damn it. Let up on the substances, you jackass. You're wrecking yourself. Tomorrow. Swear it right here, in front of the Good Lord. Pour the shit out tomorrow.*

At least the priest was nowhere around at that hour to try to give him advice he didn't want or need. It had been years since he was near the altar of a Catholic church, and he didn't want to think about that hard enough to try to remember how many.

The squat candle fell out as the cardboard collapsed in his awkward grip, hitting the floor unlit and rolling under a pew. Stifling a curse, he accepted it as a sign and left, his footsteps sharp and hollow in the empty church.

Sylvie was pacing, murmuring in a way that didn't bode well.

Stephanie looked up from the floor beside Shura's cage, regretting she'd asked her friend for so risky a favor. She felt like a clod for not registering how fragile Sylvie's connection to the real world had gotten. It was unsettling to acknowledge how shaky she was herself, right when her strength was needed in return.

Sylvie muttered something that had Ste. Anne in it, and then a chant that sounded like it was from a Sanskrit book of incantations or something equally beyond Stephanie's realm.

"What?"

"It's too late." Sylvie shook her head. "I'm in too deep. I need to lock up and be walking. Now."

"Tell me if it's too much—please." Stephanie pulled herself to her feet. "I'm never going to say you aren't the best friend I ever had, even if you decide you don't want to go through with this. I understand."

"We will do this." Sylvie wrapped her arms around herself and set her jaw. "We won't be pulled under. I don't yet have the full vision of how it will play out, but we've found a place where our minds have developed a harmonic. You believe he'll try to kill you this time, and I agree. We concur that evidence shows you might not be his first intended victim, and that the authorities are useless. You are going to have to stay aware of the way you cope by dissociating, and we'll work with that as we need to."

"You were right about the pearls." Stephanie looked down at her feet, realizing she'd left muddy footprints across the freshly waxed checkboard linoleum. "I do feel some kind of weird comfort from them, like my mother is around somehow…"

"Lucky you." Sylvie patted the tin box in her scrubs pocket. "Fortunate daughter that your mother's spirit is something you like having around."

Stephanie took her friend's hand. "To quote your favorite poet…" She rested her forehead against Sylvie's. "We both have a lot of cracks where the light gets in."

Sylvie leaned against the doorframe as she shut off the overhead fluorescents. "Ain't that the truth."

Jake looked down the long slope of the drive into Moonsong Refuge. The small herd of rescued elk, most of them descendants of bottle-raised orphans, browsed among the split-open hay bales in the feed lot by the edge of the woods. He and Duke had agreed years ago that even though they could have made good money from allowing private canned hunts, it would be a shitty thing to do. They culled and butchered the animals when they got weak, and Sarah took care of the meat and used the antlers and hides, but they didn't allow captive hunting.

As he passed the main building, he didn't see Duke and Sarah's truck. She usually went along on their rare shopping forays, and there was a spring craft festival coming up—he couldn't remember exactly when—but they'd both be gone for that too. Jake hadn't gotten a call to come take care of the animals while they were away, although he wondered if Duke would want him there after everything. No strange vehicles around and no calls meant they were probably on a supply run, which would mean he had at least a few hours to do what needed to be done.

Taking the steep, narrow track up to his old trailer, Jake bounced around and cursed that Duke hadn't graded the surface while he had the chance. It had been a freakishly mild season out there in Androscoggin County, and dry—plenty of opportunity to dump and spread a couple of loads of gravel before the rains started. Grumbling to himself, he nosed the truck into the crackling brush of winter-scorched bamboo far enough to hide it from a casual glance at the hillside from below.

The bamboo was growing right up to the trailer, dark red shoots so shiny they looked slick, reaching fingerlike a couple of inches out of the warming soil of the sunny slope. A few had already opened their first young heart-shaped, translucent mahogany leaves to the light. Japanese knotweed, as Stephanie would have reminded him to call it—not real bamboo.

*God, quit with letting her into your head. Deal with that later.*

The impenetrable clumps of brittle, segmented canes, withered and broken back by weathering to about eye level, had been parted just enough by strong defoliant during their growing season for the narrow path to the door and a few feet of cleared swath surrounding the aluminum skirting like a moat. The thicket offered privacy in exchange for the constant chore of poisoning a place to walk. New sprouts now swarmed to fill in any available spot of sun. By the coming fall, the trailer would be completely hidden.

The bamboo had never broken the surface so early. Invasive shit with roots as thick as an arm, running two or three yards underground. The canes would grow four inches a day. Tempted to kick the new sprouts down, Jake restrained himself. It was useless. The rhizome-fed thicket spread across more than an acre, and the massively interconnected entity would barely notice. Besides, he didn't want to advertise that he'd been around, even if a fresh surge of shoots would cover his presence overnight.

A ruckus started down in the kennel compound, and yowls and yaps echoed off the hill. The beasts were snarling too, like they hadn't been fed. The Gagnons were more responsible than that. It was probably nothing, but thirty or so ravenous wolf-dogs who might have scented a stranger were a distant threat still worth assessing seriously. If he didn't get it right, he wouldn't be the first illicit kennel owner to end up as dinner, nothing left of him but a few gnawed bones, and the blood licked clean.

Jake took the .22 from the glove box and fit it into the cross-body gear bag under his jacket. It was small enough not to interfere with the clambering around he needed to do, but the cheap little weapon could be lethal at short range.

Stepping between the sprouts where he could, Jake walked the familiar path with a vague feeling of unreality. The images from the hidden camera replayed on a loop in his head. Duke had carried Bree's body out—he'd watched that part over and over, her limp arms still wired together, dangling down Duke's back as he hefted her over his shoulder—but Jake had to shake off the sense that she'd be there when he opened the door.

The deadbolt balked, and for an instant Jake panicked that Duke might have changed the locks. After nervously jiggling the key a few times, he got in and turned the bolt after himself.

Everything was as he'd left it.

Behind the wood-paneled triangle where the cathedral ceiling in the living room met the flat drop ceiling over the kitchen, he knew something watched him from a drilled-out knot. The opening was an eighth of an inch, just enough to bring the tiny camera eye up to the thin plywood without limiting its field of vision. Jake had put up the new suspended kitchen ceiling that hid a partial plywood deck over reinforced joists that could support his weight. He liked being up there in the lightless, narrow place, peeking out.

Getting up into it was more of a struggle than it used to be, back when he'd first made it, before he'd even lived in the mobile home. The structure had been an office while the main building was remodeled, and he'd made the improvements on his own time, with leftover materials from the job. Now, Jake clambered onto the counter, lifted a four foot insulated ceiling tile panel beside the upper cabinets, opened the cabinet door to get a foothold, and hoisted himself inside. Kicking the cabinet shut again and setting the tile back almost all the way in so it allowed a bare sliver of illumination, he felt better—if a bit winded—lying there on his belly in the chilly, liminal space hidden between inside and out.

A few minutes into disconnecting the camera, he heard someone else fighting the balky lock.

The hair on Jake's arms and the back of his neck raised and his breath froze.

The door banged as it swung open and hit the wall. A woman's voice yowled, "You fuckin' son of a bitch, get out here! Show yourself!"

Sarah, drunk. Sarah was never drunk, not in all the years Jake had known her. She might have a beer here and there, or even throw back a shot on a special occasion, but never howling, sloppy drunk.

Motionless, Jake listened as she stormed below him, even opening and slamming the cabinet under the sink. She stomped to the back of the trailer, and he adjusted himself so he could peek out the gap in the tiles.

"You bastard! Come on outta wherever your sorry ass is hiding or I'll blast it out!"

Feeling the pulse hammering in his throat, Jake inched his hand into the bag under his arm, past the miniature tools, praying nothing would clink and betray him. If Sarah had her rifle with her, she was a formidable enemy even if she had been drinking.

"In the closet, maybe? Coward!"

Several shots resounded through the trailer. Closing his eyes, Jake counted the echoes in his memory. Three. He was pretty sure. Sarah was a straight-arrow. Five shots in a legal hunting rifle magazine.

The sound of the closet door opening, rummaging, inarticulate grief, and then a slam.

"He's not coming back…not ever. Told me it was for my own… Had to run—raked out the kiln—last thing he did—took the ashes with him… Said to tell them you found out they were fooling around an' he took off with her—and that's the truth in a way. He's a good man, not like you. They're looking for her, you lying son of a bitch! You told him nobody would give a fuck…"

Sarah collapsed in the narrow hall, her back against one wall and her feet against the other. The rifle lay across her lap. If she'd looked up and over, she would have looked right at him. Instead, she was staring at the bathroom door.

"Okay, I'll wait. I know you're in here somewhere. Didn't tell Duke she was pregnant, did you, shithead?" She waved the rifle muzzle at the door. "He had to find the fucking test in there when he washed his hands…just laying there on the fucking counter. Was that why you set him up to do your shit work for you?"

Jake flinched.

Sarah swung the rifle, but Jake fired the semi-automatic .22 first, and many times. Ten rounds to two. Two holes in the ceiling tile a few inches from his face.

He waited. No sound. He peeked out. No question. One small caliber bullet won't stop a human, but ten will, even if they just lodge in the meat. Jake didn't miss once. No inconvenient holes in the paneling from his end. He smiled and collected his cartridges with a work rag. He hadn't felt this alive in a long time.

He dragged her outside into the thicket, but left her rifle in the hall. Nodding to the little pistol, he wiped it and then tossed it and the cartridges near the body. The freezer was still full. That was good.

Leaving a dozen or so unwrapped steaks to thaw in the sun among the blood-red fingers reaching out of the ground and then down the rutted track, he left a trail from the body to the kennel building. Pausing a moment, he looked over at the elk, then opened their paddock and spooked them into the woods.

Then he opened all the cages in the kennel.

The paperwork Sylvie had sent along with the puppy's body was reprinted on a peel-and-stick label on the white cardboard box. Her heart wouldn't stop hammering. She told herself over and over that no one else could hear it, even though some part of her was sure it had to be audible to the last client of the day as she bundled up her cat into the carrier outside in the waiting room. Mercifully, the four o'clock appointment had cancelled.

The box was small, but much too large for its contents. The bag inside held barely more than a tablespoon of ashes.

*Name: [blank]*
*Owner: Stephanie St. Giles*
*Breed: Husky mix*
*Cause of death/Reason for euthanasia: Trauma*
*Biohazard: no*

Sylvie took the little box and set it inside a nicer wooden one with the veterinary office name burned in on the lid. She found herself wishing she'd let the tiny body be mixed in with the others that had been cremated at the same time, instead of asking for it to be returned. Even using the clinic account instead of billing the cost to the client, the price for an individual cremation was stiff.

Never mind. Ste. Anne had told her clearly that the puppy should be given an honorable burial where its mother could watch over it and grieve. That was the only way the ghosts could be appeased and the mother's crime laid to rest.

Sylvie's eyes were misting so badly she had to get up and walk around. She found herself staring at Shura sleeping in her cage. Making soothing sounds, she reached for the huge front paw sticking out from between the bars and examined the area around the bandage for inflammation. The wolf-dog's pads were still warm and flushed. She decided she'd change the dressing again before she went home, even though Shura was getting increasingly cranky about the process.

Shura raised her cone-collared head, started to pull her foot back inside the cage, and then sighed and left it outside the bars in Sylvie's hands. That gave Sylvie an idea.

She unwrapped the largest flattened wad of bone-white Sculpey from the euthanasia supply cabinet. Dozens of grieving pet owners had gone home with her handiwork to mark a grave or gather dust on a mantlepiece, but she'd never taken a print from a living animal. Chances were, Shura wouldn't put up with the process.

Kneeling next to the cage, Sylvie spoke in a gentle singsong while pressing Shura's paw into the synthetic clay. The dog adjusted herself to the position with another heavy sigh.

"Damn, you are a good girl." Sylvie examined the print that took up almost the whole surface of the slab. "That turned out perfect. This is going to keep your baby safe while he moves on, okay? You did what you did for your reasons, but now we have to get the ritual right to fix it."

As Sylvie put the print in the toaster oven to harden, Shura snuffled at the bars and thumped her tail once against the bottom of the cage.

As she checked the progress of the polymerizing imprint, Sylvie smiled vaguely. "I think you know just a whole lot, beautiful. I think you understand…" Turning, she stared at the animal. "Who are you? Where the hell did you come from?"

Shura struggled painfully to her feet and stared back.

Resisting the urge to lower her eyes, Sylvie touched her Ste. Anne pendant, walked to the cage and sat down by it, keeping her thoughts unspoken.

*Is your name your real name? I need to bury your child, and I have to send him out with the right songs.*

Shura burned into her with eyes the color of flame. Sylvie pressed her palms together and bowed her head in acknowledgement.

Jake's boss was in a good mood when he came in the next morning, joking about how Jake had better not share his 24-hour bug with the whole outfit.

"You can't fool me, Ferguson. You been bending your elbow too many times and wore it out." The guy was an asshole, fat and sloppy in stained coveralls, showing up after everyone else had worked out the logistics for the day.

Jake was still shaky, with shadows under his eyes and a translucent pallor, but he felt good deep down. He smiled easily and lowered his eyes. "I don't drink, Big Man. You want me to spit in your coffee to check your theory?"

Jake laughed. The other guys laughed too. He was fitting in, accepting being the new guy. Taking the ribbing with good humor. Making the deliveries to crappy locations and disagreeable customers.

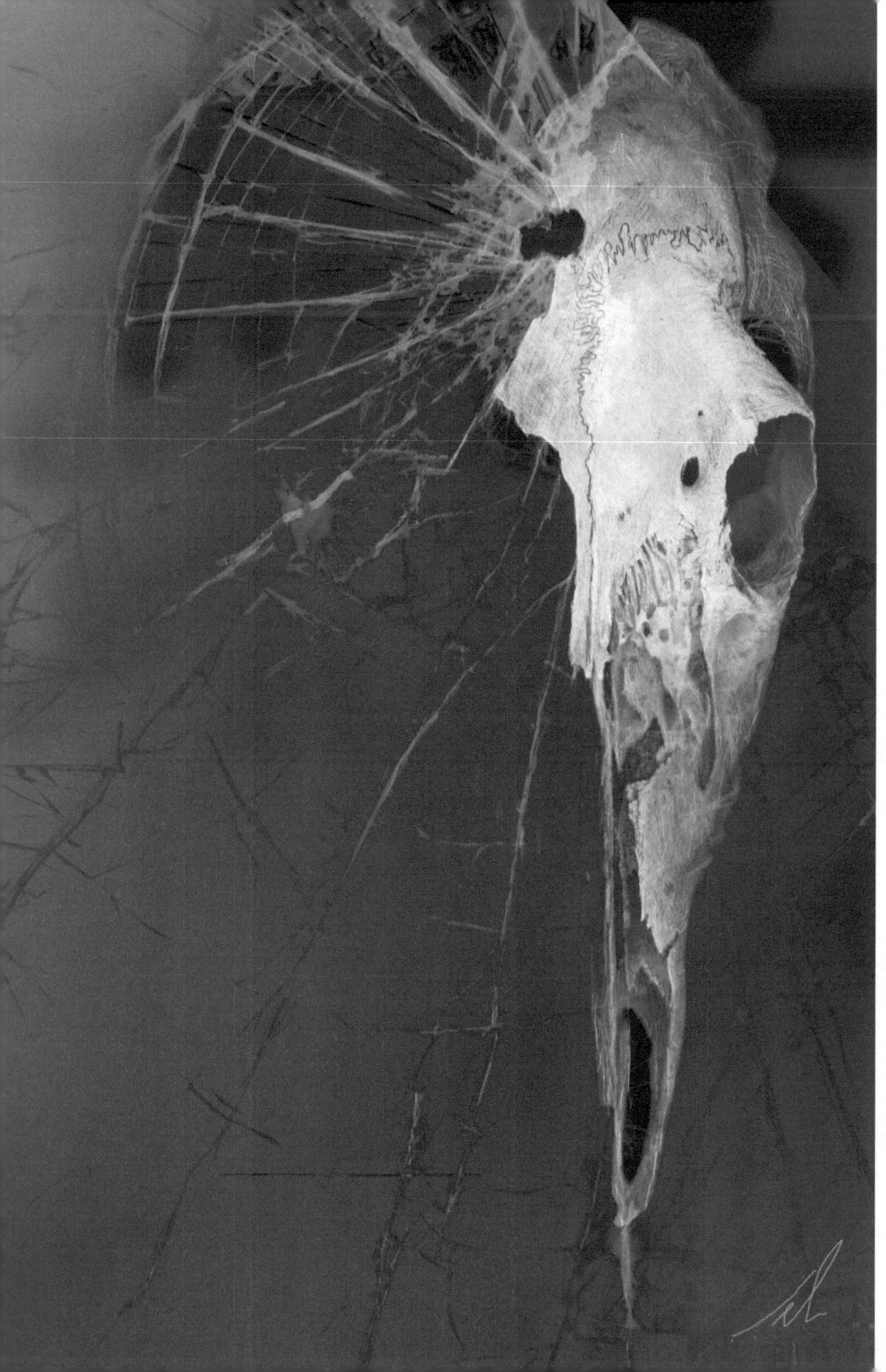

# VII

# PRAYER THAT HEAVEN WILL WATCH OVER US

UNDER THE LOW sun, Jake watched Stephanie's weird friend slog across the muddy, snow-covered field behind the clinic, carrying a funerary box and a small spade. The wind made it hard to keep the drone camera focused, and she kept looking around as if she heard something. Flapping, restless crows filled the trees around the clearing. They should have been making enough noise to cover the sound of the whirring blades, but the drone had no eavesdropping microphone to say for sure.

Through the digital eye, Jake observed as the fat woman pushed the milky white slush aside, dug a bucket-sized hole in the sodden soil, and then knelt beside it. The woman crossed herself and began rocking back and forth. She lit a bundle of twigs with pale dried leaves on them and waved the smoke around. As she picked up the wooden box, she seemed to hesitate. The eye zoomed in as she opened the box. A casting of a pawprint the size of a human hand lay on top, and Sylvie lifted it out, setting it reverently on her lap. The drone struggled to stay steady as the camera caught *Owner: Stephanie St. Giles, Breed: Husky mix* written on the smaller box inside.

The woman touched her collar and crossed herself again before putting the pawprint plaque back in the funerary box, closing it, and rising stiffly with black-smeared shins to fill the hole back in with muck.

Jake made the drone swoop away before she could look up and see it against the sky.

Stephanie couldn't shake the sense of eyes around her. When she was off the anxiety pills, she'd get sensations like that with exquisite clarity. Finally, she took the rifle and stepped out of the cabin. There were no new tracks in the drive. The softening white blanket was untouched for the quarter mile up the hill before her place, and nothing appeared disturbed beyond it. The rifle came with her as she limped around outside, but there were no signs of anyone walking there beyond deer hoofprints. The snow was starting to slump and turn transparent in the spring thaw, and the hoofmarks were ringed with ice.

Finches darted among the older trees in the small, steep plot behind the cabin, making sharp, musical communications. The thirteen wooded acres had come with the camp she'd bought with the money had mother had left for her. Her father wouldn't give it to her until after she was divorced. It hadn't been more than a few weeks later that he'd had his stroke, so something had been watching over her. Even if it was nothing more otherworldly than the intuition in her dad's decent soul, knowing he'd only recognize her for a little while longer, it was good enough, and she was grateful. She reminded herself she needed to work something out with Sylvie to board Shura when she took her monthly trip in to Lewiston to visit him.

The evergreens cast long shadows across the cabin and down the slope toward the fire road. The life-sized plastic buck archery target that had come with the property eyed Stephanie with his usual empty stare. The diagram on the hard foam insert in his side with his heart placement was gradually puffing out and eroding away where water got into the arrow holes and froze. She'd never been able to bring herself to throw him out, even though she was never going to pick up a bow.

There was a sound behind her she couldn't place, like some kind of heavy machinery in the distance, over on the other side of the hill on the Golden Road. Her stomach fluttered.

No one would be putting that kind of equipment to work in mud season. It would sink out of sight. The frost was rising out of the soil, first making it airy and crystalline and then letting it collapse on itself as it melted like overheated chocolate mousse.

Stephanie tried to locate the noise. The finches had gone quiet. Her back prickled. The Golden Road, built with private money from the paper companies during the glutted years, extended west, through miles and more miles of land sucked dry to satisfy the now-dead mills, toward the Quebec border. Once it had carried logging trucks pulling the evergreen life out of Penobscot County around the clock. She held her breath to hear a sound from it now, but it was silent.

Sometimes, when she wasn't medicated or dissociating, she could faintly hear the hipsters yelling in cleverness-inflected voices all the way from Mt. Katahdin if the clouds were low and the air was still. Sylvie was the only one who believed her when she said she could.

Sap had begun rising to feed new growth in the conifer woods, and the scent of turpentine hung there, undisturbed by invisible currents. The wind from earlier in the afternoon had subsided, but nothing reverberated along the sonic channels. Nothing emanated out of the park's scenic easement of mature woodland, or the industry's fallow feeding grounds around it.

Stephanie had to leave for Sylvie's place soon, but she didn't want to be seen doing it. The noise got louder, and more definitely coming from overhead. It was like a housefly in a jar, buzzing. She could feel it in her teeth. She rested her cane against a resin-oozing pine trunk and raised her rifle, looking for a drone. The light was difficult to sight in, strafing hard along treetops in black silhouette. She caught a glimpse of the thing and drew a bead on it, but then it shot straight up, narrowly avoiding the high branches, and was gone, taking its dentist-drill song with itself as it zoomed off.

Sylvie washed her hands in the utility sink off the surgery. The soap bubbles were silent. Stripping off her scrub pants, she gave the mud-stained knees a pre-treatment spray and dropped them in the washer. As she was pulling on her robe, it caught at her neck. When she tried to gently release the fabric, her Ste. Anne medal dropped to the floor.

Panic didn't wash over her as she thought it might. Instead, she pulled the broken chain free of her neck and pocketed it, and then bent creakily to retrieve the medal. It had landed face up.

She nodded, and a single authoritative, feminine voice above and directly behind said, "Training wheels…training wheels. *Cela est bon, fait du bien. C'est un bon plan, très inspire.*"

Wiping the medal with a polishing cloth as she walked to the kitchenette, she hummed softly.

*My priests, they will put flowers there/ They will kneel before the glass…*

Opening her purse, she pulled out the tin box and laid the medal on top of the cards.

*I summon today*
   *All these powers between me and those evils,*
   *Against every cruel and merciless power*
   *that may oppose my body and soul,*
   *Against incantations of false prophets,*
   *Against black laws of pagandom,*
   *Against false laws of heretics,*
   *Against craft of idolatry,*
   *Against spells of witches and smiths and wizards,*
   *Against every knowledge that corrupts man's body and soul…*

The words of St. Patrick's Breastplate kept running through Jake's mind. He was glad he'd turned back to his old faith. It had surprised him with its richness and support. For the third day in a row, when he came in from work, he reviewed the footage on his big flatscreen. Sylvie buried the ashes again and again. He thought about getting a drink, shook it off and smiled.

*She put my monster down. Sweet. Did it maul somebody, or was she just scared it would? How did that make you feel, Stephanie, putting her down? Hard enough for you that you had the damned animal individually cremated. Cremated. Like your precious mother. How much did that cost?*

He rewound and zoomed in on the cast of the pawprint.

*Most beautiful animal I ever bred, but fried out of its mind. Should've made ten grand out of that litter, minimum. Males would've been 150 pounds easy. Buyers lined up and a waiting list. Thanks to the witch, the whole batch went in the kiln. Except one…*

Jake became aware that he was gripping the remote so hard the battery compartment had popped open.

*Chill down, brother. Justice is coming. Maybe you let the stock get too inbred. Probably shouldn't have bred her with her uncle, but fuck her. Gave her to Stephanie and she killed her. Take your goddamned fake necklace back from the crows, bitch. Deserves to hurt like that. Only the beginning of what you deserve.*

Then he re-watched Stephanie hobbling around her A-frame shack until she realized the drone was recording her. He played it over a couple of times.

*Cute, pointing her little popgun. This is going well.*

# VIII

# PRAYER FOR COURAGE

THE GUY AT the fuel supply company sounded hungry for a new customer.

Stephanie needed to open an account and sound competent through whatever phone socializing had to be done. "I'm away a lot during the day and the tank is inside my mudroom. I can give you a key. Do you have someone who can make sure the furnace starts? It hasn't been used in a while."

"Yep. We got a bunch of keys here in the office, so put your name on it and make sure the delivery guy gives you a receipt. Basic inspection and startup—we don't do servicing. You gonna be there between noon and three tomorrow?"

"I'll make sure to be around."

"Great. Guy I'm sending over, he's a real Boy Scout. No drinking, works a couple jobs but shows up on time. You can give him your key, no worries."

Anyone in that business would expect to handle a bit of tinkering, but the extra complications would probably get kicked down to the employee with the least seniority.

*Objective one, accomplished.*

Sylvie chanted the mantra she'd been given. It was sung to the tune of *la maison Dieu* being struck by lightning.

"This. Now."

Using the passcode Sylvie had given her, Stephanie let herself in the back door to the clinic, by the exercise run. She'd stopped to clean up some droppings in there so massive that only Shura could have left them. It possibly wasn't a good sign that Sylvie had left the run un-picked-up, but Stephanie had asked her to leave it until she could get there and take care of it. She hoped Sylvie was listening to her.

She stopped to greet Shura, but the animal seemed depressed, lying in her cage and barely moving when Stephanie called to her. At least she was free of the cone. She gave Stephanie a look that said if she'd known she was going to spend her life confined like this, she'd rather have been left to drown in the ditch. There was a curve in her upper lip, showing a fraction of an inch of fang, that said she wasn't in the mood for conversation. Stephanie murmured that she'd be back, and promised the jail sentence would soon be done.

The lights weren't on in the rest of the building, even though Sylvie had said she'd meet her there. There was a soft chanting sound ahead, down the hall, that made the hair stand up on the back of Stephanie's neck.

Sylvie was rocking herself in the dark, sitting in the clinic kitchenette. Stephanie could just make out her silhouette against the moonlit window. For the last couple of days, the real world and the one in Sylvie's head had been arguing. She'd been flickering in and out of another dimension like distant radio stations arguing with each other a hundred miles from civilization.

*Objective one, scrapped. Call to cancel the delivery in the morning. No way Syl can play her position like this.*

Stephanie said, "I'm going to turn on the lights now."

"Nope."

"I'm taking Shura tonight, so you don't need to worry about that anymore. It's been a week and she needs to be out of here. I'm ditching the plan. Whatever happens, happens."

"NO you are fucking *not*. I'm bringing her to you tomorrow when you call. We agreed and you accepted my terms—no guns. You swore to me, the rifle is staying locked in your truck, and the truck is staying locked in the shed. No chance for letting things escalate. You say he's on the wagon, but you know how to prime him right—I believe you. Sometimes we have to do ugly things for the larger good. This is the impure world we live in. Like we said. So we're on."

"Syl, I'm telling you." Stephanie flipped the light switch. "I'm not putting you through that kind of stress. Period."

"Fuck you, Steve. I was just about to light a candle. This is how I pray. I'm going to show you the way to do it right, and then you're going to do it too. Now, turn that light off again, sit down, and zip it until I'm done."

The drone watched the area behind Stephanie's A-frame from its perch tucked under the roof overhang against the loosening cedar shingles. It had been tricky getting it to rest on the railing of the tiny, high deck outside the loft window. After Jake had realized the sound of its rotors had betrayed it, he staked out her driveway the old-fashioned way, waited for her to leave, and parked the little snooper where it wasn't likely to be noticed.

Its new, powerful, night-vision-capable camera tracked Stephanie as she wrestled open the sagging shed doors dragging in the wet snow, parked inside, and snapped the padlock on the hasp after herself. She'd left her rifle in the cab. Jake snickered from the comfort of his couch.

*Lock the barn door. That's right. Wouldn't want anyone to get in and plant something. Too bad the horse is already gone, and the beast has eyes on your back. He'll have the key to the house and ears inside it. Soon.*

Instead of gimping her way to the cabin, she slung some kind of bag over her shoulder, pulled out a flashlight that flared in the camera lens, and slogged up the hill through the trees. After a few minutes, the torch beam vanished, either extinguished or gone over the crest of the hill.

Jake blinked and tried to stay awake, but he'd had a long day and he really, really wanted a drink. Fighting the craving was getting exhausting. He thought he could maybe see a tiny pinpoint of light, but it made his eyes water, squinting that hard to make it out. Too tired. The kind of bleary tired he'd been the night he left the first present for Stephanie in the ditch, like he was being pulled into a void of sleep. He switched the camera off to save the battery and gave in.

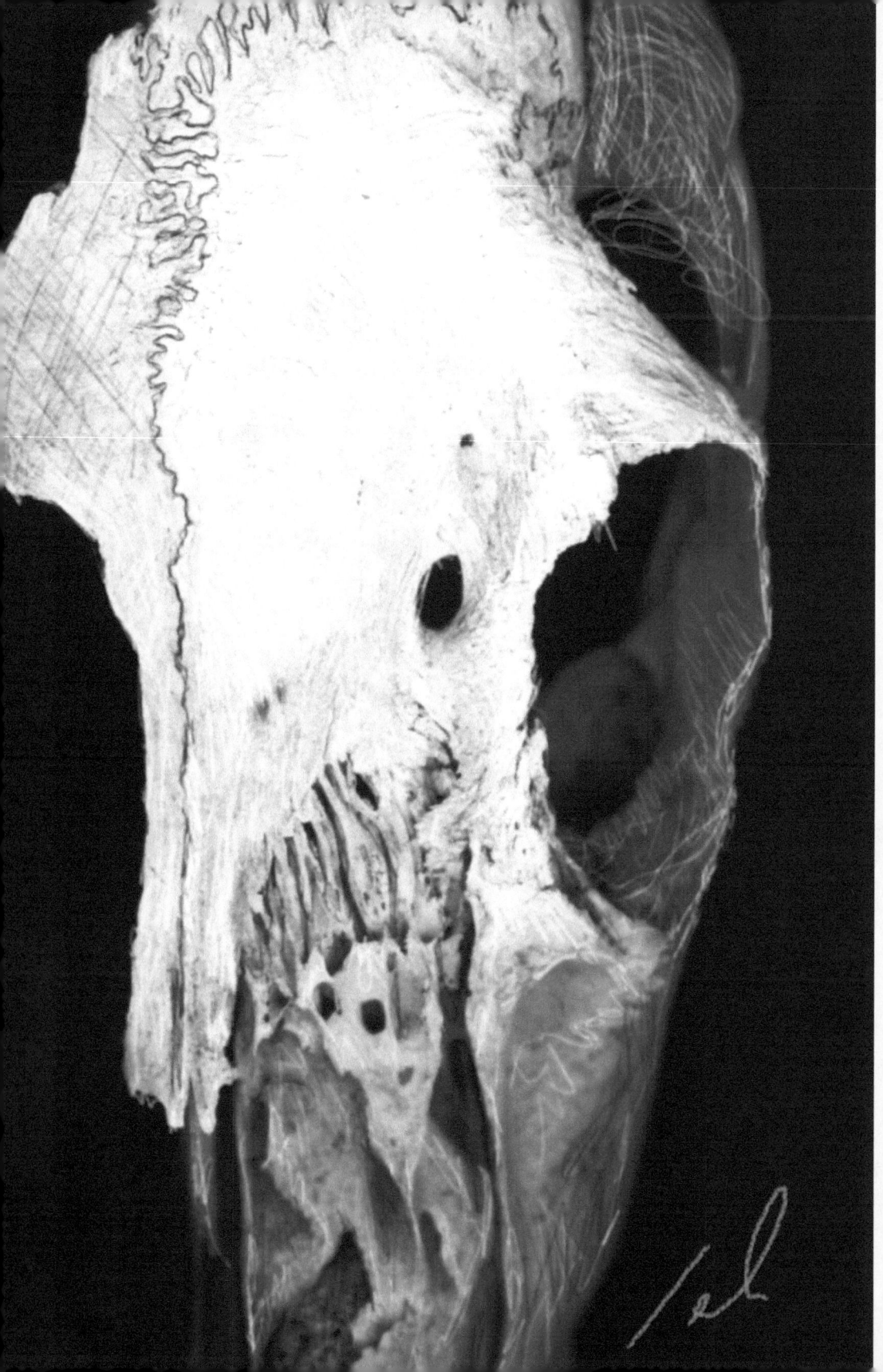

# IX

# PRAYER OF PURIFICATION

SYLVIE CAUTIOUSLY OPENED the door to Shura's cage. There was a smell about her that wasn't dog. Never having smelled a wolf, Sylvie couldn't say for sure whether that was it, but it was a scent like blood and moonlight, very faint, but very there.

Laying her hand just inside the cage, Sylvie continued her low chanting. Shura put her scarred, callused paw firmly on top of the soft human one and growled musically.

Keeping her gaze lowered, Sylvie murmured her words in a soothing tone. "Steve can get away with looking you in the eye, big girl, but I'm not going to try it again. Thank you for revealing yourself, but I'm not asking for that now. You and Steve have something going on that I can't reach. I wish I could speak the language you two share. Anyway, you're going to be free of that cage soon, and I'm going to have to be the one to deal with you, so you need to give me some deference. Not like you show Steve, but enough that we can get this done."

Shura growled again. It was a song with meaning in it, and Sylvie tried to parse the statement. The cold nose pushed gently at her face and then ran down her ear and under her jaw. Sylvie's pulse raced and she worked to keep her breathing calm.

Stephanie couldn't have said what made her choose to sit next to the buck target, but it seemed weirdly companionable there in the dark, with its bursting heart and blank eyes. There had been a new round of sloppy snow that was beginning to ice over with nightfall. A silvery beech trunk next to the deer offered a dry-ish place to sit, which probably had more to do with her choice than anything, but it felt like a fellow votary in the church of Sylvie's fracture-illuminated wisdom.

It had to have been a dozen times if it was once that Sylvie had told her the legend of the Breton seamen clinging to the bowsprit of their boat off the Gaspé, being pulled down by the storm, and how Ste. Anne had appeared to them and delivered them to safety, that Beaupré means bowsprit, and that was how the shrine got its name.

Something made Stephanie start humming.

*Until the sea shall free them…*

After lighting the candle, she set it into the clear glass chimney, burning her finger in the process, and then grumpily poked the hurt digit into the snow. As Sylvie had instructed, she held the candle aloft and sent the flickering light out into the night with the first pure, sacred thoughts that entered her mind. The message to the Grandmother of God went out on the deceptively simple tune of a mournful song whose lyrics Stephanie half-remembered from her teens, together with the relief of ice against a burn.

She took out her mother's pearls. Her father had brought them back from when he was stationed in the Philippines, and she'd always wondered if they were real. That question became the core of the ritual Sylvie divined for her.

*One way to find out.*

The necklace had an unusual design that perhaps argued for the beads to be genuine, since it used fewer of them. Each one was threaded through with what looked like silver wire with loops at each end, making spaces between them like links of a chain. The metal wouldn't burn, but the pearls would if they were fake.

Stephanie's heart was beating fast, yet she felt calm and separate from the panic. The sensation seemed kinder and wiser than just dissociation, and she decided to tell herself it was something deeper. She'd learn whether her family story was a lie, even if she'd never know whether it was her dad or whoever sold him the necklace that was the con artist. She lifted the chimney off the candle. The air was quiet and getting very cold. The area around her where she'd trodden the wet snow down was glazing over.

Holding the unfastened necklace taut at arm's length, she passed every individual pearl through the flame. Each one survived unscathed, until she got to the last, smaller ones near the clasp. She'd been hypnotized by the fire curling around the glimmering beads, and when the third one from the end scorched and shriveled, she jumped. Someone had repaired the strand, carefully matching the real with a well-made artificial version, now exposed as a sad little lump of burned plastic.

She heard a whooshing she thought was probably her own nerves in her ears. Dropping the hot strand in the snow next to the candle, she murmured something about Ste. Anne and the torrent, but she felt like a fraud. There wasn't any luminous figure made of sea spray. No vision, genuine or not.

She put on the necklace she'd just ruined to remind herself not to think she was connected to any mystical mumbo jumbo. She could barely move her legs, they were so stiff from the cold and damp.

*From here on, that's Sylvie's department. Time to get warm.*

Then the buck came apart. Not really, but the replaceable target insert where his heart had taken all those arrows popped out of him and fell onto the hardening snow with a hollow thunk. The water that leaked into him had thawed and refrozen one time too many.

*As signs go, this is about as good as you're going to get.*

Jake eyed the syringe again. He didn't want to pierce his skin with it, but he wanted what was in it to be in him. It had been a couple of decades since he'd felt that call. Maybe he'd have been better off if he just had a drink, but he was past opening the door to that temptation. The bottles were still in the cabinet—Canadian, Scotch, vodka. They could stay there, along with the beer in the back of the old, groaning fridge. No need to waste the money to pour them out. Maybe he'd have a party and share the liquor with the guys, not taking any for himself. He was immune now.

He'd have to leave for work in a few hours, and he hadn't slept. The drive into Bangor to hook up with an old contact hadn't relaxed him at all. He still felt good, just needed to come down a few notches.

Hefting the big wrench and smacking it into his palm, he contemplated bringing it down on the slim little plastic tube full of very expensive liquid, but he didn't. The heavy, oily steel was a beautiful thing, and satisfying.

The point of the needle glinted.

Shura dodged and objected vocally when the Healer tried to slide the nylon-rope training collar around her neck. It was incorrect. The Healer had deferred to her, allowing her to scent the pulse in her naked throat. She struggled with the meaning of the song the Healer had sung to her, and understood that had something to do with the wrongness. There was a part of her, the part that wanted to make the Rescuer pleased and the Healer content, that grasped the thing better. She tried to listen to it, but her body danced on its damaged legs and her jaws snapped.

Throwing herself on the slippery ground against the metal block where the Healer had cut and sewn her, she wailed and waved her paws in the air. The Healer looked down and made incomprehensible sounds, leaning in, leaving herself exposed like stupid prey. It would be so easy…

Shura didn't want to allow her teeth to do the lovely thing they pleaded for.

That was wrong. She decided.

Allowing herself to be slide-collared was against everything she'd fought to keep alive when she survived in the evil place, but things were different now.

# EQUINOX

STEPHANIE UNLOCKED THE mudroom and kept looking down the rocky hill to the lower intersection. If a vehicle took the Golden Road to the upper end of the private drive, she wouldn't be able to see it until it was right at her cabin. Her anxiety had peaked and turned to white noise. Sylvie called it post traumatic flat affect, but whatever it was, she was glad it had kicked in. She could barely feel her fingers on the door lock.

The owner of the heating oil service had called to say the guy he had scheduled to make her delivery was running late, that he'd phoned in about having a flat tire and had jumped in the tanker as soon as he got to the company lot. It didn't sound like Jake's boss was as convinced as he was trying to be convincing about the excuse.

Butterflies and caterpillars had swarmed in Stephanie's stomach until she didn't register anything but a sickish taste in her mouth.

*He'll wait until he has the key. He'll copy it and come back if he gets the chance. He's not going to do something as stupid as hurting you when his boss knows exactly where he is. For now, you're safe. You're safe. Breathe.*

Around quarter past two, the tanker appeared, coming in by the fire road. It paused for several minutes at the same spot Stephanie had found Shura, and then turned up the drive.

*Objective two, check.*

A familiar figure emerged, uncoiled the hose, and dragged it to the rusting oil tank behind the cabin. Stephanie was distantly aware of her rapid heartbeat, dry mouth, and moist palms, but she floated free of the sensations of fear. There were things she had to do to survive, and she would do them. She heard the back door open, a dismally recognizable stream of cursing, the sound of a wire brush, then hollow metallic banging followed by corroded fixtures scraping as they opened, and finally a thick liquid gurgling. She touched the damaged necklace hidden under her turtleneck for luck. Her body breathed calmly.

The knock at the door came. Jake took his cap off, wiped his hands on it and stuffed it in the pocket of his insulated coveralls. He smelled of alcohol, and his pupils were pinpoints.

"Jake—what are you doing here?" She pasted on a delighted smile. "Come on in—you're looking good."

*Objective three, check.*

*Flattery will get you anywhere. He's never cynical about a compliment. I wish it were more of a lie than it is. He takes good care of himself. At least he's honest about going bald—the shaved head looks better than a combover, and he knows it.*

"Hey, Steffie. Wasn't expecting to run into you today."

*Yeah, right. He wants that key. He saw the name on the service ticket. Something will be your fault shortly. He'll get down to the bones of you fast.*

He picked up his toolbox. "Got any biting-type animals here, anything that might run out past me?"

*Not yet.*

She shook her head.

"Getting that fucking valve open took the skin off my knuckles." He looked at his hand, aggrieved. "Used up all my rags. Now I gotta start the goddamned furnace that's probably been left to rot just as bad."

*Resist the urge to take care of him. Stay focused on the task—get him drunk, get him on the road, then call his boss and the sheriff. If he's been sober for as long as it sounds like he has, it shouldn't take a lot. Backup plan: once he has the key, get him to steal the pills while you're gone and then report it. Long-term objective: get him fired so he can't afford to stay around here.*

"I'm sorry, Jake. I can get you a bandage—"

"Nah, there's another damned thing of yours I gotta fix. Some things don't change, do they?"

*Actually, things have changed quite a bit. Appear satisfactorily chastised. Let him demonstrate his superior competence. Avoid getting him pissed.*

He cursed, twiddled the thermostat while leaving oily fingerprints on the wall, swore more and clanged his tools. Finally, the furnace kicked on, spewing a scorched cloud of dirty hot air through the registers.

*Lay out the bait.*

"Here's the key, before I forget. I'm supposed to ask for a receipt."

"Suspicious like always." He stuffed the key inside the breast of his coveralls. "Whatever—I'll get the form from the truck before I leave."

*Partially successful. Don't get sidetracked on how to prove he has a key.*

"Too bad you can't drink on the job. I got a case of Labatt Max Ice from a client last week, and I can't imbibe on this new med."

Jake plopped into the only upholstered chair. "I got time."

*Shit. That was easy. Not expected. Feels like this wouldn't be his first one of the day. Keep your guard up.*

Stephanie made as if to take a pill with water, took the six-pack from the fridge, opened one and told him he could take the rest with him. She left the thousand-dollar vial of Abilify on the counter.

Jake took the beer, drained about half the strong brew in one gulp, and wiped his mouth on his sleeve. "What's the deal with the limp?"

*He doesn't give a shit about it, except to learn your vulnerable spots.*

"Meh. I deal with it. You took care of that fast. Want another?"

"Don't mind if I do."

She gave it to him and slipped into the bathroom to give him time to check out the pill bottle. He'd know what it was worth.

Her phone dinged loudly right on time with Sylvie's text. *I'm on the Golden Road about ten minutes away.*

There were sparkles around the edges of her vision, probably, if she thought about it, because her blood pressure had dropped from a precipice, and the abyss was calling. She pinched herself on the forearm.

*Don't even think about fainting.*

From the bathroom, she announced, "Sylvie's bringing my new dog over. Can you stick around to meet her?"

*That should get him out of here. He doesn't have the balls to confront two women over an animal he hurt—never could take responsibility head on. A couple of Maxes plus what it looks like was already in him should be enough for a DUI. Give him time to reach the main road but not longer.*

As she rounded the corner, she noted the vial was no longer on the counter.

"So you lied, no surprise." Jake threw his empty at her. "You can't even take care of yourself! Where the hell did you get a dog? I been watching and seen no dog."

"I haven't heard your spy-fly around here in a week. Anyway, she was at the vet. Of course you haven't seen anything."

"Parked where you can't see it 'cause you're too stupid to know where to look. No dog. Saw your bulldyke friend bury it. Won't be scaring me with damned dog lies."

*Careful…you don't know what he might have had before he got here. The law can't get here in time. If he's left the drone here, maybe the sheriff can find it. Might help your case, but think about that later. Get him away from you. Now.*

Stephanie tried to channel Sylvie when her friend would let something terrifying and inhuman up out of her personal abyss. "A zombie dog. A huge, dead dog with yellow eyes and a bad limp. I can't wait for you to meet her."

He half rose from the chair, but then his eyes did something strange and he dropped back down.

*Oh hell. He can't go into a blackout here. He'll kill you and he won't even remember. He'll do the opposite of anything you try to get him to do.*

"Now you have to stay here, sweetie." Stephanie's palms were sweating enough that she noticed. She dried them surreptitiously on her hips behind her back. "You can't even hold a couple of beers anymore. You're in no shape to drive."

"Ugly evil old hag." He pulled his face into a scowl. "What the fuck am I doing here? There was good reason, you crazy dried up bitch. Been watching you. Can see you when you're sleeping. Yech. I came to fix something…"

*Get. Him. Gone.*

"If you can't sober up, I'm not letting you leave." She tossed the last half-inch of water from her glass in his face and planted herself in front of the door with her cellphone in her hand. "I'm calling your company."

It wasn't the way Stephanie wanted it to go, but it was the only way. She let the tension out of her body, so profoundly dissociated she knew the blows would register only as a thunderous ache punctuated by split seconds of the awareness necessary to stay alive.

Jake struggled out of the chair, staggered toward her, and swung his fist at her face.

She turned her head to save her nose, but the blow got her temple and she went down. He jerked the door open and caught her in the side with it. She registered the crack in her ribs and dove deeper into her refuge. He kicked the phone out of her grip and lurched toward the tanker.

*Stay down. Do nothing to arouse his instincts. You can't move fast enough to make it to the back door.*

A gob of spit caught her on the cheek. She remained still. She heard him turn around, and the clink of the bottles as he grabbed the partly empty six-pack. His kick crashed into the back of her head, caroming her forehead into the doorframe so her skull rang. Then the tanker door opened and slammed and the engine revved. The tires spun and caught, and the truck charged straight at the front door.

The flight of blue-painted wooden steps shattered with a grinding crunch, sending shards flying. When Stephanie opened her eyes, he was looking right at her from behind the wheel. He gunned the engine, but couldn't get traction, and backed up to take another run.

Her brain froze, wondering whether it would be better to play too injured to move or try to roll herself farther inside.

*Sainte Anne of the Bowsprit, Grandmother of God, guardian of the storm-tossed and Crone of crones, protect me I pray. I will light a candle for you every night I have left in this life.*

He gave the engine too much gas. The vehicle spun 180 degrees, ending its slide with the cab facing down the drive. The tires sprayed dirt and snow as the truck fishtailed downhill and slid off to the left, crashing.

There was silence, and then the sound of an approaching vehicle. Sylvie's SUV appeared around the hemlock stand at the curve just as Jake forced the bent door open with a grinding metallic creak. Sylvie wouldn't be able to see him from where she pulled over. Stephanie dragged herself to her knees, screaming Jake's name.

*Need to warn Syl without letting him know she's there. Keep him focused on me. Please, Ste. Anne, don't let him see her.*

He stumbled toward Stephanie, brandishing a hunting knife. She heard Sylvie's car door.

There was scrabbling, and Shura's voice. As Sylvie tried to control her, Shura put her paw over the lead and backed out of her slip collar. Sylvie held the useless leash as Shura foundered up the slope, one of her front legs barely able to carry her weight and the other only a little better. Still, she was to the threshold in three flailing, clumsy bounds.

Shura's last leap was a spinning one as she planted herself in front of Stephanie. Stephanie willed her all her strength, putting her hand against the animal's heaving ribcage so Shura could feel the whispered words. "Baby girl, it's going to be your teeth versus that knife. I'll do whatever I can to make it a good fight. I love you."

Shura's voice was a low, singsong snarl. Jake reached the broken base of the steps, with only a steep eight feet between them, and he leaned forward to get a handhold on the stony slope.

Sylvie was behind him, tiny and plump in her tweed city coat and her turquoise Totes boots and matching driving gloves, holding up her little emergency-kit hatchet.

*Oh hell—no, Syl, no. You can't take him. You don't know what you're dealing with. Stop her, Ste. Anne. Make him look at me. Please, please, please. She can get away if she runs right now.*

Stephanie screamed, "NO!" but Sylvie swung at the back of Jake's head, an expression of lethal concentration on her face.

He stopped climbing, turned, and dropped to his knees, the knife slipping from his hand. Then he lay his face in the mud, the pink-handled hatchet wedged at the base of his skull. Red began streaming downhill. He didn't move. Shura sang softly, the fur on her back straight up.

Sylvie stood motionless as she and Stephanie stared at each other. Then Sylvie stepped carefully around the blood, picked up Jake's hand, took the knife back and slashed her coat from the shoulder to the elbow, nicking her skin so it darkened the fabric. She replaced the hand and knife back precisely where they had come to rest.

Shura sat down.

"I'll go with her assessment that it's safe." Sylvie nodded toward the dog. "Your back door unlocked?"

Stephanie croaked out an affirmative.

Sylvie circled around the cabin, and Stephanie heard her come in the mudroom. Pulling herself inside, Stephanie called Shura in and pushed the door closed from the floor. She couldn't reach up to bolt it. Breathing was like trying to swallow fire.

Sylvie leaned over her to throw the latch and then slid to the floor with her back against the door. "Anything I need to say or not say when I call the sheriff?"

Her voice rasping, Stephanie whispered, "No. Just not…that I brought him here."

"Yep. You saw me pull on his arm to stop him, right? He turned on me with the knife. Close your eyes and see it happen."

"Okay." Stephanie curled around her broken ribs. "Are you sure he's…"

Shura lay down next to her, gingerly sliding to the floor on her damaged front legs.

"I wouldn't have tried that if he didn't have a bare head." Sylvie rubbed Stephanie's shoulder gently. "Medulla oblongata severed at the atlanto-occipital. Business portion of the guillotine cut. Controls heartbeat and breathing. He's gone."

Sylvie pulled herself up, walked stiffly to the landline phone and called the sheriff's department. Stephanie thought she sounded saner than most people. The conversation had words and phrases like "self-defense," "stalking," and "ignored our previous reports."

Drifting in a half-conscious daze, Stephanie blinked and then her head lolled. Her ears roared, and there was a swirl of misty aquamarine light. She heard Sylvie saying something about being a nurse and needing to check on her.

Sylvie hung up and came back, lying with her head pillowed on Shura's shoulder. Tight, quiet sobs came from her, and then she rolled onto her side and took Stephanie's hand.

"I need to fall apart for a little while, Steve. Lot of fractures in the looking glass. Lot of blood."

"Not a problem." Stephanie opened her grip on her ribcage just enough to let Sylvie slide her free hand under to hold her arm. "I made a promise to your saint. You have votives?"

"Always." Sylvie's voice cracked. "I'm scared, Steve. Pray for me. For real. I need to come off sane or they'll 302 me again."

Stephanie brokenly hummed the song she'd started when she'd fire-tested the pearls, the words in her mind circling around to the beginning again.

*And you know that she's half-crazy but that's why you want to be there…*

The soft sound hung over them like soothing tears. Shura heaved a deep, satisfied sigh.

"That's a good one." Sylvie closed her eyes. "Lot of people when they hear it think Our Lady of the Harbor is Liberty in New York, but she's not. She's Mary, Star of the Sea…Notre-Dame-de-Bon-Secours Chapel, Montréal. On the way to Beaupré." Sylvie nuzzled against Shura. "I'll put our girl in the bathroom while they're here. You need X-rays and then you'll stay at my place for a bit."

They waited for the sirens.

# ACKNOWLEDGMENTS

Particular thanks to my faithful East End Writers, Paula Martinac and Lucy Turner, who put up with me until I got an idea of what I was doing. Once I did, hindsight still makes me wince to think of what I put them through. No writing of mine, including this small book, would exist without their mentorship.

Thanks also to Scarlett R. Algee of JournalStone for taking in this little stray and giving it a good home.

# ABOUT THE AUTHOR

Selene dePackh is a queer, physically disabled, neurodivergent crone who forefronts marginalized characters and subjects in her work. Until recently turning to writing, she worked primarily as an illustrator. Kirkus describes her 2018 debut novel *Troubleshooting* as "a gripping, lyrical, and ambitious dystopian novel," whose lead character is one of the "few protagonists in sci-fi—or literature in general—that present an autistic perspective with such specificity and pathos."

Her short genre-fluid speculative fiction has recently been included in *The Nightside Codex, Recognizing Fascism, Nightscript,* and *Oculus Sinister* anthologies, among others. Her essay on online friendships among autistics appeared in the Identities issue of the British litmag *Shooter*.

www.ingramcontent.com/pod-product-compliance
Lightning Source LLC
Chambersburg PA
CBHW030237180626
46810CB00008B/3178